Addicted to Him

Addicted to Him

-Written By-

Linette King

Copyright © **2015** by True Glory Publications

Published by True Glory Publications

Join our Mailing list by texting TrueGlory to 95577

Facebook: Linette King

This novel is a work of fiction. Any resemblances to

actual events, real people, living or dead, organizations,

establishments or locales are products of the author's

imagination. Other names, characters, places, and

incidents are used fictitiously.

Cover Design: Michael Horne

Editor: Artessa La'Shan Michele'

Acknowledgements

First and foremost I have to give all thanks to God.
Throughout all of my trials and tribulations although I

didn't know it then, I know now that he never left my side. I could have been dead and gone a long time ago when I woke up and couldn't breathe. Turns out I had several blood clots in my lungs and had God not Awaken me I wouldn't be here today. Thank you God for everything you have done and everything you're about to do. Continue to shield and guide me as I embark on this new journey.

To my children: Aaliyah, Alannah and Jaye: I love you. Never let anyone tell you anything different. All of these hours I work and every book I write is so you won't have to go through the struggle I've gone through. You can do anything you want; all you have to do is put your mind to it and never give up! Never back down or run away from your calling.

To my family: Mama I love you and all of your craziness! I still think you need counseling though lol. I remember you use to tell me so many things I didn't understand when I was younger but I want you to know I heard you loud and clear and I understand now!

Mr. Terry, my dad, I know it's not biological but you've always treated me as though I am actually your daughter. I'm forever grateful for that. My biological father hurt me deeply when he left but God sent you to me because he knew I needed you! I love you!

Pooh, everybody's favorite person, my sister, I'm thankful to have you in my life! You and Oliver have literally been my rocks! I love yall so much!

Lorenzo, my brother, my protector, I love and miss you so much! I wish you were closer or that we had more time to visit one another more often. Congratulations on your new addition!

Oliver (Tunky), Omarion, O'lasha, O'Ryan, O'brien, O'daysha, Ocean, Kamaria, Jacolby, Mhainami, Amina and Karlie I love you guys! Never forget it!

To my extended family: My second mama, my kids call her Sweet Mama, you are truly a blessing to have! I can talk to you about any and everything! You do so much for my children and you don't have to but you do! Love ya bunches!

My first lady Nicole, if it weren't for you and Pastor Willis I'd probably still be saying "I'll get saved next Sunday" lol. Ever since I got saved blessings have been raining down on me. Thank you for always lending a listening ear and being such a great role model! I love you!

Jasmine! The best friend any girl could ever ask for! My children's Godmother! My Day 1! One of the only people I can talk to about anything and when I say anything I mean ANYTHING! Lord help us because some of those conversations are TMI! I could go on and on about you but your head is big enough! I love you Jazz and no matter where life takes us you will always be my friend. Even though I'm not too fond of Lucy!

P! Precious! The only person that calls me "Lil Baby" lol Girl I don't even know what to say about you! We got each other through plenty of nights working in that ER girl! I miss working with you and Patty Wagon or you and Deaunda! We were the A Team! Anyway I've known you since Elementary but I'm so glad to have a friend like you.

Trinisha! The circumstances behind our friendship would lead someone to wonder why we ever started communicating in the first place but I wouldn't change it for the world. Had those events not taken place I'd be short one good friend. No scratch that one great friend! You're freaking awesome and I love you! You're living proof that you can know someone all of your life and meet someone new who has better intentions for you than them! Never change! Well make some adjustments because you're crazy! Take care of Payton and MJ!

To my readers; I hope you enjoy this book and become a fan of mine! This is a work of fiction. Just a story. If anything seems like I could be talking about a specific event or individual it's purely coincidental.

ADDICTED TO HIM

Rashard

The guys and I are walking through campus before practice, about to watch the girls on the track team do their thang, when I spot ass. See, when ya boy spots ass, I be on it. I leave Dre and Twan, my teammates, and head over to see what the face looks like that's connected to this ass. Oh yea, I'm Rashard Peterson, number 06, quarterback for UMA. This is my last year and I'll have my Bachelors in Business

Management. I do my thang with Twan and Dre in these streets too.

If you want some weed, I got you, but that's pretty much all I'll touch. I never keep enough on me to get a charge. The most I'll have on me is a blunt and shit, that's for recreational use. Ya boy ain't dumb by a long shot. That's why I got this degree in the works, so I can open up different businesses.

Anyway, if you want pills then holla at Twan; my boy got opioids, tabs, Xanax bars, and Prozac. This nigga even got fentanyl patches for some of the people at our school that can't swallow pills.

Now, if you want anything else, Dre got it and if he doesn't have it, then he can get it. Dre's ass knows every fucking body. He's the only nigga I know that has white, Hispanic, and Asian friends.

"Damn bruh, look at the bih over there!" Twan said, putting his arm in front of me, like I was gonna haul ass over there once I looked at her. Too bad for Twan cause I was already looking. I never seen her before, but um, shawty was bad. We all stopped as we watched her lil sexy short ass stretch, getting ready for her race. I did the Heisman on Twan's ass, making him side step, and jogged up behind her.

"Say ma, what's your name?" I ask, licking my lips because this bitch is looking good as fuck. The closer I get to her, the more impressed I am. I can tell that her ass is fat and her waist is small, and since she's only wearing tights and a sports bra, I can see that her titties ain't big. My only thing is I'm not use to dating dark skinned bitches. They have too much attitude for nothing, just like this bitch because she hasn't even acknowledged that I'm standing here! Not to be conceited, but ya boy got it. Shit, I'm 6'2" and dark skinned. I keep my dreads fresh by getting them twisted once a week, and I stay in the gym. I know I'm the shit because these bitches be flocking! That's why I fuck 'em, dodge 'em, and keep it moving.

"So, you're just gonna ignore ya man?" I ask. I watch as she inhales deeply, then turns around looking like I slapped her damn mama. See what I mean? Dark skinned bitches just be mad for nothing!

"My man?" she asks, and I'm thinking, *bitch, not for real.* See, I think all dark skinned females are bipolar, and I'm waiting on her to go from attitude to happiness to crying because that's what they be doing. Bitches got no fucking guidance.

"So, what's your name, Miss Lady?" I ask, completely ignoring her dumb ass question. Of course, I didn't really mean I'm her man, but I couldn't walk up saying, 'Girl you bad and I wanna fuck', now could I?

"Tamia. Tamia Anderson," she answers like she's nervous or something, so I know I got her. I can't lie though, she's the first dark skinned chick that didn't give me any attitude, so I'm interested. She stuck her hand out like I was gone shake it! Ha! My first thought was to grab that ass and pull her to me, but I decided to be more respectful because like I said, these dark skinned bitches crazy! And when I say bitches, I mean no harm. Anyway, I grab her waist and pull her to me, and she stands there long enough for me to know that I can fuck.

"Um…guy. I don't know you, so keep your damn hands to yourself if you wanna keep them hoes!" she says, shocking the fuck out of me because even though I'm use to dark skinned chicks with attitude, it never be that bad with me! Shit, it's me! Rashard mother fucking Peterson, quarterback for UMA! Bitches be trying to get with me and here I am, getting handled by a dark skinned bitch! The best thing for me to do is walk away.

"My bad, Miss Lady. I'm Rashard. Give me your phone, so I can put my number in it," I say because looking into her beautiful big eyes, I can't just walk away without trying. For some reason, she stares at me for a few seconds, then that unfamiliar look becomes all too familiar when I realize she's choosing. Bitch bold because when she gets down to my dick, she just stares, like its gone hop off and run away and she don't want to miss it.

"You gone give me ya phone or stare at my dick all day?" I say and smirk at her, but she's literally still staring at my dude. *Fuck it,* I think to myself because I can see that big ass phone in her track bag. I reach down and grab it, but the shit is locked.

"What's your code?" I ask because if she gonna be on my team, I'm going to need to know it anyway.

"Nigga, I'm not giving you my damn code! What's the point in having one if I'ma give it to every silly mother fucker that asks for it?" she says, rolling her neck. And there it is! That attitude that people say black women have! Are y'all born angry? I swear, I have never met a happy black woman before. She gotta be rare as fuck because I only come across these bitches with attitude, and I know they all haven't had a fucked up upbringing.

Before I can respond to her, her Coach is calling her to start the race. I walk off to find Twan and Dre, and they're in the stands ready to watch the race, so I head up there to 'em.

"You got your ass handed to ya, didn't you?" Twan asks.

"Naw, she's mine. She just doesn't know it yet," I reply.

"Nigga, you bugging!" Dre said laughing, and I just shook my head.

I can't wait til football practice is over, so I can go chill or something. A nigga been up running around all day.

POW!! The starter shoots the gun, and the race starts. I keep my eyes trained on Tamia. Her stride is on point, but I don't know why she's doing the 100-yard dash with no speed. She's doing good though, keeping up with that other chick. I jump up when she passes her but then, she slows down and I'm like, what the fuck yo!

"GO LEXUS BABY! RUN!" I heard a lady yelling, and I assume that she is the one that's picking up speed. Tamia is good, but that damn Lexus fast as fuck. It's like she lets you take off so you can think you're about to win and be like, 'lemme quit playing with these bitches', and go ahead and pass you up. Needless to say, Lexus won and the lady is up here going crazy.
I can still hear her screaming as I make my way back down the bleachers to the field.

"You did good, Miss lady," I say to Tamia, walking up to her.

"Fuck off!" she yells and takes off running into their locker room. I started to yell, *Bitch if you would have taken off like that in your race, you would have won hoe,* but I didn't. Fuck her.

After football practice, I went home to take a shower and laid across my bed thinking about Tamia until Tiffany called, asking if she could come through.

Tiffany is one of my jump-offs, but I never fuck her. I just let her give me head. I fucked her one time and her pussy game was poo. The shit wasn't gripping or leaking, but her head game is on point, which is why I keep her around.

Thirty minutes later, Tiffany shows up with an all-black lace thong and bra set with a sheer teddy on top of it. See, this another reason why all she can do for me is suck my dick. Bitch will go outside like this and think I'm going to add her to my roster? Naw, fuck that!

She walks in slowly with some high ass red 'fuck me' heels on and my dick immediately sprang to attention. I let her push me down on the couch after pulling my shorts and boxers down because this is her show now.

I watch as she pulls my nine-inch-thick dick out and make that mother fucker disappear! It takes everything in me not to moan out like a bitch. I ought to kick this bitch in her face for sucking my dick this damn good! She goes from sucking dick to licking my balls. Then, she hums with my balls in her mouth and jacking my shit off at the same time! I swear, she's the truth. She leans back up and deep throats me again, and I feel my nut rising as my dick jumps in her mouth. She starts sucking real fast then she moves to the head, sucking hard and jacking off the rest. Now, a nigga's toes curling. I think I died twice when I released in her mouth and she swallowed it all like a champ. I just closed my eyes ready for a nap.

I felt this bitch sliding a condom down my shit! "Oh no ma'am, you know that ain't what we do," I say, pushing her away from me and snatching the condom off my dick. Bitch thinks she's slick trying to wait until I was dozing off. "Get yo ass out!" I say and push her towards the door, before she can fix her mouth to say anything.

"Come on Shard! Why you always doing me like this when you know I love you!" she screams.

"Love these nuts!" I say as I kick her out my damn house for playing with me. Now that that's over, I can take my ass to sleep.

Tamia

Honestly, I knew who Rashard was before he told me. He was extremely popular because of athletics, football to be exact. I just didn't have time to be another notch on his belt. See, I'm what I like to call a "good hood bitch". What I mean by that is I have book and street sense. I start no trouble but if you bring it to me, then you better be ready because ya girl TTG! (Trained to go) I was taught to always be ready so you never have to get ready. I'm 5'0", small breasts, and got a waist that's screaming *FIND ME,* which is making my ass look bigger than it is. I run track for UMA, which is how I met Rashard, officially anyway.

"Say ma, what's ya name?" I heard someone call out as I stretched, getting ready for my hundred-meter dash. I literally hate for someone to call me ma. I don't know why these bitches keep giving birth to these niggas. I say bitches because women have gentleman, ha ha. Some logic.

"So, you gone ignore your man?" This time, I stood upright because he was closer. This nigga just called himself my man and I'm thinking, *where the fuck they do that at?*

"My man?" I asked with my lip turned up and giving him attitude for days. See, I gotta give a nigga attitude that look like this because my panties got wet, on the slick. I ain't trying to be fucking this nigga under the bleachers. Um, because I will. It's been four years since I had sex because my ex-boyfriend, Amere, cheated on me.

"So, what's your name, Miss Lady?" he smirked, completely ignoring my question. When he licked his lips, gosh, they were full and plump! That fat pink tongue made my clit jump and I had to cross my legs.

"Tamia. Tamia Anderson." I respond, sticking my hand out to shake his, but he put his strong hands on my damn near invisible waist line and pulled me in for a hug. If my panties weren't wet a second ago, then them bitches are drenched now! I look into his eyes and roll mine inwardly as I step out of his embrace and remove his hands from my waist.

"Um... guy. I don't know you so keep your damn hands to yourself, if you wanna keep them hoes!" I say with a twist of my neck and turn to walk away, only for him to grab my wrist softly. The look I gave him caused him to put both hands in the air as he laughed the sexiest laugh I ever heard.

"My bad, Miss Lady. I'm Rashard. Give me your phone, so I can put my number in it," he stated, shocking the fuck out of me. Normally, these niggas can't handle my mouth and once I give 'em attitude, they go from 'excuse me miss' to 'fuck you then bitch' or my favorite, 'you ain't shit anyway'. But not Rashard's sexy chocolate ass. No, he doesn't care about all that mouth I just gave him. I allowed my eyes to travel all over his smooth chocolate skin. He has hazel eyes, perfect teeth, full lips, his dreads are freshly twisted and the way his sweatpants are hanging around his waist loosely, leaving nothing to the imagination, is doing something to me. I'm literally standing here, staring at this man's dick print.

"You gone give me ya phone or stare at my dick all day?" he asked with a smirk, snapping me out of my dicknopsis state. Yeah, I made that shit up. What else would you call being mesmerized by somebody's meat? Then, this nigga's cocky and I'm loving that he's straight up, but I'm hating it too because this nigga's fine as fuck. If I'm digging him now, after only a couple of minutes of conversation, what will I do if he fucks me good?

I guess Rashard figured I wasn't moving fast enough because he reached in my Nike one strap track bag, pulling out my IPhone 6. "What's your code?" he asks.

"Nigga, I'm not giving you my damn code! What's the point in having one if I'ma give it to every silly mother fucker that asks for it?" I reply because this arrogant ass nigga is starting to piss me off.

"TAMIA! LET'S GO! IT'S NOT TIME TO GET A MAN, IT'S TIME TO RUN YOUR DASH!" Coach Gray yelled at me from across the field, embarrassing the fuck out of me. I didn't even respond. I just turned to walk back to the line, so I can get another stretch in before it's time to run. I'm running against Alexus Jones and Kylie Hunter. Kylie has the fastest take off but Alexus catches a strong wind towards the end each time, and my stride remains the same from beginning to end. I really don't think I should be running the hundred-meter dash; I'd much rather do third leg in relay.

"RUNNERS TO YOUR MARK. GET SET." POW! We're off.

Of course, Kylie takes off and she's in the lead, but I'm right behind her. She starts to slow down and I pass her right up. I glance to my right and I can see Alexus has caught her wind, and she's gaining on me. I started running harder but it doesn't feel like I'm going any faster. I can see the finish line and feel the sweat dripping down my neck. Rashard's dick print comes to mind and a slight tingle goes down my spine. "GO LEXUS BABY! RUN!" I heard Alexus' mom yell, snapping me out of my daze and I began to pick my pace back up, but it's too late. Once Alexus passes you up, it's over with. SMH.

"Fuck!" I yell, after crossing the finish line seconds after Alexus. I could have had this bitch! Man fuck, I been working out so hard in between classes, and I still didn't win. I always come in second! I can hear my cousin, Armani's voice in my head right now, *well at least you didn't come in last.* I always hate when she says that. Just because I didn't come in third didn't make me any better than Kylie.

"You did good, Miss Lady," Rashard said, walking up to me.

"Oh, fuck off!" I say as I storm off in the direction of the locker room.

I walk in the locker room and just start throwing shit everywhere! I'm kicking and punching doors because I'm really pissed off! Nothing I do is ever good enough. I try my best in everything and it's never good enough! I study my ass off for exams and still never get an A+. I work out and train Monday through Saturday, and I still never come in first! "This is some straight bullshit!" I say as I throw myself on a nearby bench and place my head in my hands.

I look up, while running my hands through my hair, at the sound of someone clearing their throat but I don't see anyone. I'm honestly glad I don't because I was so close to crying and even though a tear didn't fall, I know my eyes are bloodshot red because my hands are trembling and my legs are shaking. I grab my bag and head for the door.

"If you want to beat me, you have to be the best. And since, well um…" she paused as if in thought, "I'm the best, then it will never happen," Alexus said with a huge smile on her face.

"Bitch, did I send for you?" I ask because I may not have won that race, but I will beat this bitch's face in right now. See, I'm from the coast! And baby, on the coast, if you come for someone that didn't send for you, you're liable to get that ass popped on the spot!

"Bitch? Who the fuck you calling a-" I punched the bitch in her mouth before she could even get her question out. She stumbled backwards into a wall of lockers and slid to the floor, holding her mouth and nose. Coast folks don't do no talking. These bitches keep coming for me and I can show them all better than I can tell 'em.

I watched Alexus for a second to see if she was going to get up so we can fight but she just sat there, looking dumb as fuck, trying to catch all the blood that was dripping. I mean, come on now, bitch! As flip as her mouth is, I know she done fought someone before, but she sitting here scared of her own damn blood! Like really? Get up and fight or get up and get a towel. I back pedal out of the locker room because I'll never turn my back on someone I just hit.

Once I make it to my little Honda, I head to my 2-bedroom apartment I share with my cousin, Armani. We are both from the coast but neither of us start shit with anyone. We're two of the coolest females you will ever meet. Armani is bad too, just not as bad as me. Well, of course I'ma say that, but giving props where props are due, she's bad. See, I'm 5 feet even and dark skinned, not black but um, maybe brown skinned with small breasts and a big booty. It's really not even that big, it's just that my waist is small, so it gives the illusion that it's bigger. Then you have Armani, light skinned, big tits, and big butt too, but I mean her booty is dumb! I've never honestly seen a booty that big on a light skinned chick. Come on now, how many light skinned chicks you know have ass for days? Scratch that, *real* ass for days? But then, she has gut. I guess she's one of those BBW's Drake be talking about in his songs (Big Beautiful Women). Now, don't get me wrong, her gut is because of her choice of food and lack of exercise but hey, to each its own, right?

Anyway, by the time I make it home, I'm dog tired and just want to hop in my shower and go to bed. But, as soon as I walk in, I get pissed! There are clothes leading to Armani's room and I just know she has another one of her sponsors over here. Armani uses men to pay her half of the bills, while I use my refund check from school and the money I get from doing hair in my free time. This is why my closet looks starved and hers has overflowed into the hall closet.

I, immediately, start picking up the clothes they had taken off and thrown on the floor, folded them up and sat them outside of Armani's door. I could hear the moaning and for the first time ever, I listened. When I bent down to sit the clothes outside the door, I realized it was cracked and I could see them.

By no means am I into females, but like I said, it's been four years. I got all the way on my knees as I watched him slide his big black dick in and out of Armani. Her moans were a definite turn on and I could feel my clit jumping again. He grabbed her bra and snatched it off, tossing it to the side in one quick motion.

"Tell me what you want," he says, slapping Armani's big ass, leaving his handprint on each cheek. The impact causes me to jump back, but I quickly gathered myself.

"Fuck me harder, daddy! YES! PULL MY HAIR!" Armani yells. See now, this bitch is a freak! I never know who she's fucking because she calls them all daddy.

"Like that baby? You like that?" he asks.

"Yes daddy, but fuck me harder! Tear this pussy up!" she moans, as he began to ram his dick in her, causing her body to shudder.

"Mmmh," a soft moan escapes my lips. I didn't realize I had stuck my fingers in my panties, massaging my clit as I watch.

"Put your face in the covers and toot that ass up higher," he says as she rotates with him still in her. He pushes on her back, so she could lower her head. He raises her ass a little higher and sticks his tongue in it.

"Oooh, you nasty fucker! Do dat shit, daddy!" Armani says as he continues to stick his tongue in and out her ass with his dick still in her. I start circling my hips faster and before I know it, he is sitting upright, fucking the shit out of her with his thumb in her ass and watching me play with myself. Once I notice he is watching, I start to slide my hand out.

"Don't move!" he says

"Ok daddy, I'm bout to come again" Armani replies but he's looking at me, so I think he's talking to me, but I'm not sure. I'm frozen.

"Keep doing that shit!" he demands and I slowly start winding my hips on my fingers. "You like this dick don't you, sneaky bitch?" he says, sliding in and out of Armani slowly.

"Yes daddy!" she says as I nod my head slowly.

"You want this dick sneaky, bitch?" he asks, still fucking Armani.

"Yes daddy! Aaaaagh!" Armani yells as I nod my head.

"Well, cum for me," he says and as if on cue, my body shudders, my clit jumps, and I rub harder and faster. I cum right there outside the door, watching him fuck her as he watches me. They both cum shortly after, and I hurry and catch my breath and run to my room. A shower is really needed now.

Armani

Yo! Armani Wright here! See, I was the baddest bitch on the coast and now, I'm the baddest bitch in Detroit! Standing at 5'3", I have big tits and ass for days, baby! I'm light skin with long black Brazilian weave and bright red tips. See, I know what I got and I know how to use it to get what I want. Back when Tamia and I were on the coast, I worked at Cookies and Cream. I was smaller than I am now, so it worked out better. I have a little bit of gut now, but I still can get any man I want. These niggas ain't shit and these bitches ain't either, which is why my circle is so small, it's damn near nonexistent. My only friend is Tamia. She's the only person that was there for me when my mama's boyfriend kept coming in my room.

Every night, through my sophomore year in high school, he would bring his dumb ass in my room. I remember the first time he came in, he told me he was tired of me walking around teasing him. Yeah, I wore crop tops and booty shorts a lot but damn, I was only sixteen! Granted, I've had the body of a Goddess since I was thirteen but fuck; I was only sixteen! I hadn't even began having sex yet when this perverted ass nigga came in and stole my innocence! Every time he would come in he would say, *Don't ever give my pussy away.* I told my mama and she didn't believe me! I told Tamia and she had me dress in all black, and we met at the factory he was working at.

"Mani! What's been wrong with you?" Tamia asked. *"Nothing,"* I replied, still looking off into space. It had been a few months since Steve took my virginity and he had been in my room every night since then. It

had only been two days since I told my mother, who damn near slapped the skin off my face before calling me a liar. "Bitch, I know you! Now, tell me what's wrong? You been walking around like your puppy died," Tamia said. I started to cry and when I mean cry, I was sobbing. When I looked up, Tamia was crying silently while watching me. She sat there staring at me, waiting on me to finish crying. "He raped me," I said with my head down after I got my breathing under control. "Who?" Tamia asked. "My mom's boyfriend, Steve." And she walked away. I started crying again because I thought I lost my best friend. A week later, I received a text message from Tamia telling me to meet her at the factory downtown and to wear all black. I knew it was Steve's place of employment and being hip to the game, I knew something was about to go down. I just didn't know what.

So, when I get there, Tamia is already there waving me back towards the back door, so I head that way. "He comes out here every night at 10:30 to smoke a cigarette," Tamia says quietly. I pull my phone out to check the time and it's 10:20, so I'm nervous. I haven't seen him since I told my mom what he did. Whenever he comes in my room, I don't look at him. I keep my eyes closed the entire time! The night I told my mom was the first night he didn't come in my room, since it all started. But the very next night, he fucked me so roughly; I wished I hadn't told a soul.

"Come on, get down over here," Tamia said, pulling me near the dumpster. Together, we crouch down on the side of the dumpster. "Put your hood on!" Tamia demands. A few seconds later, we hear the back door creak open, and Steve walks out and turns towards the street with his back to us. Tamia stands and it's the

first time I notice that she's holding a bat with rope wrapped tightly around the handle and nails going through the other end of it. She walks up to Steve and whistles once she's in arm's length. Steve turns around and before he can say anything, Tamia swings the bat in an upward motion between his legs. She then hits him two times in the face and I notice she has on brass knuckles. Steve falls to the ground with a pained expression on his face. He's crying. He's pathetic. I slowly stand up and approach them. Tamia and I look at each other and without saying a word, I grab the bat and snatch it from between his legs. Blood goes everywhere as he lets out the most horrific scream I've ever heard. I raised the bat above my head and swung with all my might over and over and over. I hit him between his legs for every night he came in my room and raped me! I hit him until I couldn't hit him no more. "Damn bitch! We were just gone beat his ass, not kill him!" Tamia said, snatching the bat from me. That's why I love her. We didn't kill him, I did. We left the coast together and moved to Detroit, Michigan.

I walked in the two-bedroom apartment I shared with Tamia and realize, Tamia must have cleaned up before her track meet. Tamia's always cleaning up and fussing, but I love her to death. She's like the mother out of the two of us. She had one boyfriend named Amere all of her life, so he's the only person she ever been with sexually. But me, I been giving this pussy away to any nigga with a fat wallet. I ain't ashamed neither! See, some of y'all hoes be in denial but please believe, if you gone call me a hoe, you can't say broke first. Meanwhile, you bitches fuck any nigga with tattoos or dreads, and that nigga be broke! So, before you judge me just know, I'm living in luxury sitting on this fat ass and even fatter bank account, while your broke ass sitting there reading this book! Oops! I tried it! Ha!

Dave: Are you busy?

Armani: Never too busy for you, daddy

Dave: Are you home?

Armani: Yes. Swing through

Dave: Iight bet.

Now a bitch is super excited because I saw this Gold and Black MK bag at Saks that I've been dying to get, and he's just the sponsor to go get it. See, I keep them coming back because I don't ask questions. I don't pout when they leave. I listen to them when they want to vent. Of course, my pussy game on fleek and I'll suck ya soul outcha through ya dick!

Good thing I don't have to clean up because Tamia wakes up every morning faithfully, cleaning up. She even cooks breakfast and dinner. Neither of us is ever home during lunch time. Anyway, all I have to do is hop in the shower and get ready for Daddy to come.

After I finish my shower, I go in the kitchen to get my pineapples out of the refrigerator. See, pineapples are a permanent fixture in my diet. I eat them every day because it keeps my pussy juices sweet. Daddies tell me all the time how sweet it is, so it's my job to keep it that way. Daddies meaning all of my sponsors. There's only four: Dave, Vincent, Zach and the other one doesn't want anyone to know, and being the perfect chick that I am, I have told no one!

Knock! Knock! Knock! I swing the door open because I already know it's Dave. He barges in, kissing me roughly as we pull each other's clothes off, tossing them on the floor on the way to my room. We enter my room and he uses his foot to kick the door close. I back away from him and do the come here motion with my finger. He pushes me back on the bed and stands there staring at me, taking me all in. He then leaves a trail of kisses, softly sucking my skin each time from my ear to my waistline.

I'm laying across my bed anticipating his warm mouth feasting on my love tunnel. I can feel his breath as he lightly blows my clit, sending chills up my spine. He starts to kiss my inner thighs, getting closer to my girl but then, he moves away teasing me. I swear I want to punch him on the top of his head.

"C'mon daddy!" I beg.

"Tell me what you want."

"Taste it," I reply, and he slowly sticks his tongue in and then goes right back to my thigh.

"Dammit, why did you stop?" I whine.

"You said taste it. Tell me what you want!" he demands.

"Devour this pussy daddy!" I moan. He dives in without missing a beat. He's licking, sucking and slurping all on my girl and before I know it, my legs are shaking. He grabs them, locking them each under his arm and holding me still as he continues to eat me into a frenzy. In one swift motion, he flips me over onto my stomach and starts fingering my girl with his tongue in my ass.

"You love me?" he asks before sticking his tongue back in my ass.

"Yes! Daddy, I love you!" I reply because I can't think straight with his tongue in my ass. I would've said anything he wanted me to.

He removes his fingers and slam his dick in me, then pulls it out and pops my pussy with his hand before slamming back into me. He did this three times then pulled out and stuck his tongue back in my ass, and I came every fucking where. We continue to fuck for the next hour. It wasn't until he started calling me a sneaky bitch that I realize he must have found out about my others.

See, all of my sponsors think they are the only one. It's my job to make them feel special, so I go along with everything they say. The only thing is if they find out about each other, then I'd end up having to find new sponsors or getting a job, and a bitch like me was not taking the ladder.

"Don't move!" he says.

"Ok daddy, I'm bout to come again," I reply because at this point, I have to do whatever I need to do to make sure he doesn't suspect anything.

"Keep doing that shit!" he demands, and I'm confused because I'm not anything but being still. But hey, when your pussy is this good, you don't have to do much for a nigga to think you're doing the most. "You like this dick, don't you, sneaky bitch?" he asks, sliding in and out of me slowly.

"Yes daddy!" I scream because out of all four sponsors, he's my runner up!

"You want this dick, sneaky bitch?" he asks, fucking me hard. I mean, this nigga is long dicking me!

"Yes daddy! Aaaaagh" I yell, feeling my body quiver.

"Well, cum for me," he says. I have the most intense orgasm ever! I'm spent.

I lay there in a daze, watching Dave get dressed. That's my only problem with him; he will fuck me silly then leave me wanting more. He says him and his wife are going through a divorce but the way he runs out of here after we're done suggests otherwise.

See, as I said before, I'm not a dumb bitch. Growing up in the hood with more guy than girl friends, put me up on game. I see right through these niggas, that's why I always say these niggas ain't shit but these bitches ain't too far behind.

"I'll get up with you later, alright," Dave says.

"Ok daddy," I smile.

"This why I always come back. You don't give me no mouth or ask no questions, but that soon to be ex-wife of mine will nag a nigga to death!" he says while approaching me. He bends down and kisses my lips. "Keep it tight for me!" he says over his shoulder.

"Alright Daddy, lock up on your way out." It wasn't until I heard the door close and what sounded like the shower water cutting off, I realize Tamia must have come home while I had company. I know she's going to be pissed because she hates it when I bring sponsors home. She always giving me hell about how unsafe it is but hell, I know everything there is to know about my sponsors, in case they try anything slick. I have a copy of their social security cards, driver's licenses and birth certificates, thanks to my girl Tiffany that works down at the medical records office. I have detailed descriptions of their body written in my journals. They each have their own journal where I write everything they tell me, whether it's personal or public, legal or illegal information. I also have all of their information saved on a disc drive and cd drive. Hell, they each have a folder on my google drive! So yeah, like I was saying before, I'm far from dumb.

Michelle

Hey, I'm Michelle Melton. I'd like to say I'm a pretty chick. I'm slim, standing at 5'4", and light skin. I keep my hair cut short like Bird off of that old movie called *Soul Food.* I've been dating Ray for about 6 years now on and off. We have our problems just like every other relationship, but we're still going strong. I work at this bar and grill called *Carte Blanche.* The owner Raphael named it that because it's one of those *anything goes* places.

The place looks small on the outside, but it's huge! It actually put me in the mind of an old hole in the wall juke joint from the outside. You walk in and the bar is to the right, stretching across the entire right side wall. In the ceiling on every corner is a cage with a dancer in it. Now, that's one job I couldn't do. Can you imagine being extended in the air having to dance all night? Naw, I can't, which is why I'm a waitress. All of the regular tables are placed strategically around the room. Raphael doesn't leave anything to chance, so I'm sure they are placed the way they are for a reason.

Anyway, there are four VIP booths that you have to be escorted to because there is a secret elevator with a different code for each booth. I have no idea how to get to the secret elevator because only certain waitresses know about them. I only know it exists because I asked Candy, who just so happens to be one of those waitresses. I was asking because I always see people in those booths, but I never see how they get there or how they get out. All I know is from the floor I can see the surrounding VIP booth glass, which looks like a bubble with its patrons inside living it up.

There's also a ground level of the bar and grill called *The Basement*. It's where Raphael has employee meetings, meetings with friends and where he hosts dog and chicken fights. The dog fights are normally held on Wednesday and Thursday nights, and the chicken fights are every other Saturday. I've never seen either fight because only certain waitresses get to host those fights.

I try not to ask Raphael for any extra jobs here because he's such an ass! I've been taking dance classes, so I asked Raphael if I could apply for the cage dancer position and he said, "How da fuck would it look for me to have yo skinny ass up there dancing?" Since I didn't have an answer, he walked away. I know I said I can't imagine being up there dancing and I couldn't, until Candy told me they make five stacks a night! I can for damn sure dance and hold my piss all night for five g's! It's probably good I didn't get that job though because Ray would leave my ass for sure if he knew I had started dancing here. He already didn't want me working at a bar anyway.

Ray and I have a date today, but I haven't been able to get in touch with him. It's Thursday, and I'm positive I will see him Saturday because that's the only day I do hair. Yea, on my quest to figuring out what I wanted to do with myself, I went to hair school and Ray paid for it. I been doing hair every Saturday since graduation. I can do anything but I only do five heads, starting at 8:00am. I try to get my sew ins out of the way first. I have a few regulars and they occasionally will send someone my way.

Anyway, Ray and I go through this a lot. Sometimes, he's feeling himself a little too much and he will start fucking off with someone else, but he always finds his way back home. Regardless of if he fucking off with someone else or not, I still see him every Saturday faithfully, so I know it's something there. Always have been and always will be! He hasn't broken up with me yet, so I don't know why I haven't heard from him today. I've been calling and texting him all day. I know he's busy but damn, I'm his future, so the least he can do is make sure I'm ok.

Whenever he would do these disappearing acts on me in the past, I would pull up the *find my phone* app on ICloud and go to him, but he's figured out how I did it. I'm pissed because I have no idea how he knew! Hell, I hadn't told anyone that's how I had been finding him and I learned how to use the app after my cousin, Tiffany, showed me. That bitch is so good at finding shit out that she might as well get paid for it. She's so messy though! I don't understand how someone so pretty can be so messy! Then, she has all of these children that should keep her busy enough to not be in any mess, but she never has them.

Tiffany is indeed a baddie! Growing up with her was so hard because I've always been skinny, and she's always been curvy. She always got all of the attention too. Not only was she a redbone but she had ass for days and no stomach! Her downfall is she's ratchet with five kids and four baby daddies. Her ass been trying to lock down a baller for years, but it ain't working for her. She used a turkey baster to get pregnant the first three times, but last time when she got pregnant with the twins, she poked holes in the condoms. It took her a few months to get pregnant with the turkey baster each time, that's why she tried something different with this last guy. I've never actually met any of the dads, but I can tell by their living situation that she doesn't have any help.

Tiffany lives in the 39th street projects. They call it dead man zone because of the high numbers of smokers walking around. The smokers be high and leaning so far over, I just know they're going to fall, but I've never actually seen one fall. Anyway, she has a three-bedroom project home. Her rent is seventeen dollars and the project manager write her a check each month for her power bill. The water is included in the rent and she receives food stamps. I wish I could get some but I make pretty good money, not to mention Ray doesn't allow me to want for anything.

Tiffany: wyd bitch?!

Michelle: just got home from work

Tiffany: heard from Ray yet?

I can never trust that she will keep my business to herself so anytime I can, I just ignore her. I know it's a reason Tiffany is texting me and more than likely, it's because she knows something I don't. The last time she texted me about Ray it was because she saw him with another chick at the mall and wanted to know if we were still together. Boy, I tore Ray a new asshole after that and it was only three weeks ago and he's disappearing again! I'm just going to ignore her because Ray and I are supposed to be going out tonight, and I don't want her to ruin it.

About thirty minutes, a shower, and nap a later, I wake up and check my phone. Do I really I have to tell you that there are no missed calls or texts from Ray? Guess I should just call him.

So, I've officially lost my cool after the tenth call that went straight to voicemail, and I start throwing things around my small but cozy one-bedroom apartment.

Michelle: I'm done.

I texted Ray because I am so over his bullshit! I should not have to constantly put up with this from him. I've been riding for Ray for 6 years, and he still puts everything and everyone above me. I'm so freaking tired of it. I want so badly to cut all ties with him! I'm finally going to let go because I can't keep going through this with him.

Ding! My text message tone interrupts my tirade, causing me to pick my phone up and launch it across the room! I watch as it hits the wall and shatters into about as many pieces as my heart has been broken into. Instead of sitting around sulking, I decide to turn on Mary J. Blige and clean up the mess I made.

Two albums later, I'm done cleaning, washing clothes and putting them all up, so I decide to grab my Kindle Fire and read a few books.

Knock! Knock! Someone knocking on my door interrupts me from my book and I was just about to find out if the main character's boyfriend was alive or not. *Knock! Knock!* Ugh! *Whoever it is will just have to wait until I finish this chapter*, I think to myself as I continue reading.

Before I'm even on the next page, I can hear the locks on the front door unlocking and knowing it's Ray, I jump up and run to bathroom to check my face. Besides the puffiness around my eyes from crying, I look perfect. I washed my hair today and let it air dry and my natural curls are on point, so I know he won't be able to resist me. I quickly spray a few squirts of Love Spell on my neck and inner thighs, wash my face, and head out to see why Ray had been ignoring me.

I bet you sitting there like, this bitch just said she was done but hell, the heart wants what the heart wants. I know Ray breaks my heart over and over, but he's the only person who can make it feel whole again! I love him more than I love myself sometimes! Hell, we should be married with kids by now, but Ray wasn't ready to be a father when he got me pregnant about three years ago. I remember it like it was yesterday…

Ray and I had been going hard for each other for three years. Friday nights were our date nights and he would let me choose where we went. Well, this particular Friday, we had just spent the night before making love until about 4 am. Knowing the next day was a big day for us, I planned his surprise down to the T. See, I had been sick for weeks and my period was late, so I already knew what time it was, but Ray however, had no clue.

"Wake up baby," I said shaking Ray but he didn't budge. "Ray, baby. Get up!" I said a bit louder. I needed for us to be on time or this wouldn't be a surprise. Since I couldn't get him up by talking and shaking him, I went under the covers and took his dick into my mouth. "Mmmh," Ray moaned and adjusted his body in the bed. Whenever he turned slightly to the side, I knew he was about to fuck the shit out of my mouth. So, I relaxed my throat muscles and clenched my jaws, so it would be tight for him and he could still go deep. I had to learn which direction to turn my head whenever he would pump to match the curve of his dick.

"Shit girl!" Ray moaned, slowly pumping in and out of my mouth. I allowed him to make me gag so more saliva would produce, making my mouth even wetter. "Aaah fuck, Chelle!" Ray yelled out as his dick slightly jerked in my mouth. Anytime I felt that jerk, I knew he was almost there. I slowly massaged his balls as I sucked harder and faster until he released down my throat.

I hopped up and went to brush my teeth, since I had already showered. Once I was done, Ray was sitting up in bed with a smile on his face. I walked up to him and kissed him on his lips with his morning breath and all. I loved every bit of Ray and I had no problem doing anything he asked me to do.

"C'mon take a shower baby, I have a surprise for you," I said. "Is it anything like what you woke ya boy up to?" Ray asked. "It's better!" I said excitedly as he got up to take a shower.
Twenty minutes later, we pull up to this building and there were no other cars visible to us as I parked my car and we hopped out simultaneously.

"What you got going girl?" Ray asked slowing his pace. "If I told you, it wouldn't be a surprise now, would it?" I responded. Even with Ray being hesitant, I'm still excited because I know once he sees his surprise, he will be ecstatic!

I open the door to the building and flick the lights on as everyone jumps up screaming surprise! I mean, it's beautiful in here. There's a banner on the back wall saying 'Congratulations' and one hanging in the center of the ceiling, welcoming us to parenthood.

It wasn't until all the smiles disappeared that I turned to see Ray, walking back to the car. Embarrassed, I ran out of the door behind him. "What the hell Ray? Where are you going?" I asked, once I caught up to him and grabbed his arm.

"Who the fuck pregnant?" he screamed at me and I can understand why he's mad. He wanted to be the first person to know about it, but I told his family and friends first and planned this party, instead of sitting down so he wouldn't be blindsided like this.

"Me, Ray! I went to the doctor to confirm Wednesday," I explained but he's just staring at me shocked because he's excited. I mean, he's literally standing in front of me with his mouth wide open.

"I'm ten weeks, baby!" I said now jumping. I can no longer contain my excitement. "By who?" Ray asked and now, it's my turn to look shocked. Oh my, have the tables turned! I'm now looking at him and I can only imagine how wide my mouth is because my jaw has got to be resting on the pavement by now. Ray is the only man I've been with in years! We've been dating exclusively and he wants to stand here and ask me who I'm pregnant by! Oh, I'm furious and I just want to slap fire out of his ass for embarrassing me like this!

"Bitch, you're tripping! I ain't get yo ass pregnant! I wrapped up every time and checked the condoms each time! The fuck you thought I was doing in the sink every time? I was making sure yo ass ain't poke holes in my shit!" he screamed at me. Ok, maybe he's right; he never actually nutted in me per se. Maybe I did go about this completely wrong. I just didn't think he would react this way! I was tired of not having a title and I so desperately needed one.

"Take me home, Bo," Ray said to his brother and that's when I realized the party had come outside. Everyone was just standing there looking at me. I could hear the whispers and giggles now.

"Fuck!" I said to myself as I made my way to my car without even talking to my party guests. As soon as I left, I called the clinic to schedule an abortion. When I got pregnant, it was because I wanted to be more than just the chick Ray was screwing. I had hopes the baby

would bring us closer but it only tore us apart. That Monday, I called Tiffany and had her come with me to the clinic to get my abortion done. Ray didn't answer any calls or texts for two months and when he did, he didn't even ask about the baby.

"Why yeen text me back or answer the door?" Tiffany asked, jarring me from my daydream of the past.

"Ugh! What are you doing here?" I replied, flopping down on my sofa.

"I knew you were over here crying, so I came to get my favorite cousin outta her funk! Get up, let's go hit up the mall," Tiffany said. Instead of arguing or trying to fight it, I simply got dressed and headed out the door.

Rashard

So, when I woke up from my nap, I had 32 missed calls and 108 text messages. The text message that stood out the most was the one from Dre telling me the trap had been hit! Fuck! Man, ain't no way the fucking trap got hit when we move the mufucker every three days. I hit Dre back telling him to set up a meeting like yesterday!

We all meet up in *Dead Man's Zone* where I keep a house up, just for us to pass through. When we reup on anything, we meet at what we call *The Cave,* to separate everything before distribution. Nothing stays here long. I make sure everything is in and out within three hours and not only just here, but all of the trap houses. I'm the only one that knows where all the product and money is held because I don't trust anybody that can see, hear or talk. A mother fucker can see you do something and hate on ya; they can hear about your come up and plot against ya; and shit, we all know loose lips sink ships! Now, I know I downplayed myself like I just dibble and dab here and there, but truth be told, I'm running the streets of Detroit!

Going to school and playing ball are just decoys. Who would expect a broke college student to run the biggest drug empire Detroit has ever seen? See, I'm not flashy or flamboyant and even though Dre and Twan are my dudes, they don't know I'm the boss. None of my connects even know I'm the boss! See, what I do is send different runners to pick up different products from different connects; that way, I'm not tied down to one connect.

No runner brings me anything directly, they each have a drop off spot that only them and myself know about. When they show up to drop off the product, I already have their payment there, so it's an even exchange. The drop off is simple. I text each runner from a different burner phone every other week saying, **I'm in need.** This means, go see your connect. Each runner always sees the same connect because most connects won't do business with any and everybody. So once a bond is made between runner and connect, that's their guy. Anyway, after the runner gets the product, I receive a text saying, **it's a go**, meaning I've received your product and I'm heading to my drop off spot. I don't respond to that text, I just go to my safe house and count up enough to reimburse them for the product and pay them handsomely for their services. After the runner drops the product off and grabs their bag of money, I receive a message simply saying, **thanks.** After that, I delete all text messages, remove the battery and sim card, burning them and the phone in my incinerator. I bet you're wondering what a nigga doing with an incinerator! Well, I do a lot of things and no evidence, no crime. See? Simple.

Since I trust nobody, I'm never there for the exchange but I'm always close by, in case one of these niggas get ballsy enough to take my product and money and leave. Anyway, once they're gone, I go in through my underground passageway to get the product and take it back to my safe house, which is where everything is. Each drop off spot is connected by my underground passageway, so I can get to each spot swiftly before the runner has a chance to do anything fishy.

I trust Dre and Twan but not with my life, that's why they don't know they work for me. They think we all are just small time dealers, trying to make a way out of no way while in college. I'm a firm believer that two can only keep a secret if one of them is dead and I'd hate to have to lay one of my boys out.

I pull in *dead man's zone* in my fully loaded 2014 black on black Honda Accord. Like I said before, I'm not flashy. This car is good on gas and the police pay ya boy no mind. I'm zooming through the fiends and see a familiar face sitting on the porch of one of the other houses. I thought she moved out. I told the bitch last week if she wanted to stay on my team, she had to move out! Bitch ain't listening, so she gotta go! One of my jump offs already live out here, Tiffany stays right on the corner when you first pull in through the first entrance.

When I met Chardae, she was like a breath of fresh air with her light complexion, long brown hair with blonde highlights, hazel eyes and the right size everything! Her titties weren't too big or too small, and neither was her ass. When I first saw her, I was in awe! A nigga almost wanted to settle down! Then her sex game was on ten! What made me change my mind about wifing her was that she sucked no dick! She ain't ever want to clean or cook shit! Then, she still lived with her mom. Not only that, but the bitch had no goals in life! She was perfectly fine with letting a nigga take care of her.

"What took you so long?" Dre asked, walking up to my car. I hadn't even realized I was at *The Cave,* thinking about Chardae's fine nothing ass.

"Bruh, what da fuck happened, yo?!" I asked, ignoring his question because I'm here for one reason and one reason only, and that's to find out who's a fucking snake in my camp. See everybody think the boss put me in charge of this trap, they don't know I am the boss.

"Man, all I know is I came to drop off some skittles for Smurf's ass, and this lil nigga was laid out on the couch and all the shit was gone!" Dre said, pissed off. See, now I'm pissed because I stay telling these little niggas to stay on their game! I ain't got time for shit to be getting hit! I'm seriously not trying to be doing this shit all my life. A few more years and I want to be out but set for life, now this nigga, Smurf, done set me back!

"Where that nigga at?!" I ask heated as I pull my dreads back into a ponytail. Dre turns and walks towards the house, and I follow suit. I follow Dre through the house down to the basement were Smurf and two other niggas sat, tied to chairs. See, Dre and I are always on the same page. For him to already have these niggas down here means he feels it's a snake in our camp too. Dre and I share one glance before we walk completely into the basement.

When I walk around the chairs, I can clearly see who's tied up now. Smurf, Lil Devon, and Chris are all sitting here mugging me like I'm the one robbed them! Shit, they should have been guarding my product with their lives! These three niggas were assigned to this house for this rotation and out of three, this is only the second day. Nobody knows about the rotation except for the workers I choose to work it, Dre, and myself. So, in order for the trap to be hit on the day that Dre was supposed to drop off five pounds of skittles, it's looking real fishy. For those of you that don't know what skittles are they are LCD's; pills that causes you to have hallucinations. I have no idea why anyone would want to take something that causes you to have hallucinations but hey, if they will buy it, we will sell it.

"So, you niggas decided to steal from us?" I ask as I pull out my toolbox. I turn to look at them after I get no response and they are glancing at one another, waiting on the other to speak. I catch Dre's eye and nod, giving him the signal. He walks up to Smurf and hits him in the chin so hard, teeth and blood sprays out of his mouth. Without missing a beat, he walks up to Lil Devon and Chris, doing the same thing.

"Whose idea was it to rob us?" I ask as I set my drill up and make sure the battery isn't dead. When I look up, they are looking at each other again. I catch Dre's eye and he pours gasoline all over Devon. By this time, I have my drill ready to work.

"Was it yours?" I ask Lil Devon as I kneel down in front of his chair with my power drill. I look up and watch as Lil Devon's eyes get as big and round as saucers.

"Naw man, I ain't have shit to do with it!" he screamed.

"Well, who did?" I asked, turning on my power drill. Everyone looked on because nobody knew what I was about to do. I slowly drilled a bolt into each leg of the chair. I bet your wicked ass thought I was about to drill Devon! Well, ya boy can't stomach torturing mufuckers!

I bolted all 3 chairs down into the basement floor, so no matter how much they rocked, it wouldn't fall over. I needed them to be as steady as possible. Allowing them to rock out of the chairs could easily give them a chance to turn the table on us. If they were smart, they would have tried the shit and hauled ass while Dre was out front waiting on me. They could have easily rocked over, causing the chairs to break, and wiggle out of the ropes, which is why I'm about to tape their little asses down! I don't care how hard you wiggle, your ass ain't wiggling out of gorilla tape.

I move back to Devon, taping both wrists around the arms of the chairs. I tape his ankles around the legs of the chairs, then I move to his torso, taping him steady against the back of his chair. I toss a roll of gorilla tape to Dre, so he can do the same with the others. Once everyone is tapped and secure, I nod towards Dre and he walks to the back and get the flamethrower.

Meanwhile, my phone is vibrating. I pull it out and answer because it's Ma Dukes. "What's up ma?" I answer coolly.

"Nothing baby, just checking to see if you're coming over to eat Sunday?" she asks.

"Yes ma'am," I respond. Every Sunday, the family meet up at my mom's house after church and eat dinner.

"Are you going to bring someone this time?" she asks. My mom has been pressuring me to take these bitches serious but they don't have all of the qualities I need them to have in order to take them home, so I don't.

"No ma'am," I said.

"Baby, I'm ready to have some more grand babies," she says because my sibling's kids are getting bigger.

"I know ma, look, I gotta go. I'll see you then ok."

"Ok baby," she says and hung up.

I watch as Lil Devon, Chris, and Smurf look at me like I'm crazy. I run up to Chris and hit him over and over with the butt of my gun, screaming "Who robbed you?!" Before I know it, I done beat Chris to death and I'm no closer to finding out who the snake is.

"Man, I don't know what you're talking about. I was in the back when the shit went down," Devon said, shaking his head at me. I look to my left and Dre is waiting on my signal. I nod towards Dre and he walks up to Devon with the flamethrower and lights his ass up! I watch as he tries his best to break free of the tape but to no avail. I grab the extinguisher and put the fire out. The smell of burnt flesh fills the room, making my stomach turn. I turn, heading up the stairs after nodding at Dre.

"Shard man, wait! Don't leave me with him, man. It was some bitches came in here and caught us slippin!" Smurf yelled, halting me in my tracks.

"Yall let some bitches rob y'all?!" I asked.

"Yea man," Smurf mumbled with his head down.

"Who?" I asked, walking back towards his chair.

"Man, I'on know, but they were bad as fuck! We ain't know they were packing heat til it was too late, man. They got everything and left. We were in here drinking and shit; they must've drugged me, yo! I'm sorry man, just don't leave me with him," he pleaded, gesturing towards Dre.

See, these niggas let some bitches come in here and catch them slipping, when those bitches shouldn't have even known what was in here. I bet them niggas were bragging and shit! That's what I get for hiring young niggas. I nod towards Dre and walk out of the basement. I could hear Smurf's screams before I ever even made it out of the house.

Like I said, my stomach can't handle torturing someone, but Dre's ass loves it! If anybody knows how Dre gets down, it was Smurf's ass, which is why he was basically begging me to kill him, instead of Dre. Had he told me all of that before I killed his boys, I would have killed him instead of Dre, but since he wanted to play tough in front of niggas that were about to die any fucking way, I let Dre have his ass.

Tamia

After eavesdropping on Armani and one of her sponsors, I took a shower and went to sleep. It was the first time in a long time that I got some good rest! I didn't wake until about four hours later, and I was home alone again. I got out of bed and made my way into the living room to find something to watch on Netflix. Once I settled on catching up on *Revenge*, I headed into the kitchen to make me a sandwich. I promise, every time I walk in this kitchen after Armani has been in here, I get mad! Man, I love Armani to death but she needs to work on being more clean! When I say I do everything here, I literally mean everything! I get up every day and cook and clean. I keep the clothes washed, even hers because if I don't wash her clothes, her room will start to smell.

I remember when I went on strike a few months back, the odor that came out of her room was indescribable. No female should ever smell like that! Ever! I made her wash her own things that week, and she forgot about a load of clothes and left them in the washing machine for a few days. Man, no lie, when I opened the washing machine those clothes were so sour I washed them twice, then cleaned the machine out.

As I look around the kitchen right now, I see she fixed her a plate of what I cooked earlier today. She must have eaten twice and used two different plates. She does that dumb shit! Anyway, she also fixed herself some Kool Aid and wasted a few drops of it on the counter. Now I'm really mad because that red Kool Aid will stain damn near anything! All she had to do was wipe it up as soon as she spilled it instead of leaving it there for me. I don't even want her washing dishes because when we use to take turns washing them, the ones she washed would always still be greasy, even the cups! Now, why the fuck are her cups greasy?

I get busy cleaning the kitchen then head into the living room to start on *Revenge*. About three episodes in, I hear the front door unlock followed by Armani entering a few minutes later.

"What's up, chick?" Armani asks, flopping down next to me on the couch.

"Nothing," I respond dryly.

"You been in the house all day, Mia?" Armani asks and I know she wants me to ride somewhere with her. Armani can't understand that I'm a homebody. If it wasn't for school and track, I would never leave the house. I'm perfectly fine sitting on this big comfy sectional watching Netflix. Instead of answering her, I focus my attention back on *Revenge*.

"C'mon, ride to the mall with me," Armani says. I get up slowly to throw some clothes on. Since I have no one to impress, I throw my long hair into a messy bun on the top of my head. I put some gold hoop earrings in my second hole and cubic zirconia studs in my first hole. I put on a fitted white crop top shirt, skinny jeans rolled up right passed my ankles and finish my look off with a gold belt and gold sandals. When I make it back into the living room, Armani has changed as well.

Not the one to let anyone outdo her, she's dressed like a million bucks! She's wearing a Michael Kors asymmetrical all black dress with gold trimming. She has her long weave pressed bone straight with a slanted part in the middle. I can't see her earrings but she has on a gold plated necklace with her name on it, a gold ankle bracelet that says loyalty, and black and gold Michael Kors sandals. Armani is always camera ready! Before she comes out of her room in the morning, she combs her hair down and throw on something presentable for company, even when it's just us. I'll never understand it but hey, to each its own, I guess.

"Ready?" Armani ask, applying pink Mac lipstick to her lips.

"As ready as I'm gonna get," I reply as we head out the door.

"Mia, can I ask you a question?" Armani asks.

I'm really like here we go but I say, "go for it." She unlocks the doors to her 2013 cocaine colored Cadillac Escalade for us to enter. We both hop in and pull off before she continues.

"You're a really pretty girl, Tamia. Why don't you keep yourself up? Do you want a man?" she asks, stunning the fuck out of me. First of all, I'm beyond pretty! Second of all, niggas be falling all over me, so I must keep myself up good enough! Third of all, fuck no, I don't want a man! Niggas are too much trouble! I'm just trying to keep my track scholarship, so I can continue going to school to become a healthcare administrator. So um yeah, having a man is the least of my concern.

"I keep myself up well enough and no, I don't want a man. I don't need to lose focus," I reply. I know you thinking, *bitch you were Billy bad ass a few seconds ago* but you don't know Armani. Now, don't get me wrong, I'm not scared of nobody that bleeds, but this bitch is crazy! If we go toe to toe, I can take care of her no problem but since we've moved to Detroit, she done got on another level. Armani keep razors stashed all over her body and you won't see it coming. Plus, arguing with her while she's driving is committing suicide. She will turn to you to snap back without pulling over or anything, so yea, I'm playing it safe.

"Sometimes well and well enough is all I'm saying Mia," she replied, clearly aggravated.

"Just drop it!" I demand. The rest of the trip to the mall is a silent one.

We parked on the side of *Devonshire Mall* with the food court, so we could eat once we finished shopping.

As soon as we got out, I spotted Lisa Cunningham walking into the mall. "When did she move here?" I ask Armani, pointing in Lisa's direction. I looked up to see Armani shooting daggers at her and shrugging her shoulders.

"Do you think he moved here with her?" Armani asked.

"I sure as hell hope not! I don't want him trying to come back in my life causing mayhem! I am finally over him and I don't need him coming around causing me to backslide," I replied

Before Armani could respond, I grabbed her hand and started back pedaling to the car. I felt like my heart was about to burst open. There was a huge lump in my throat and my vision became blurry from the tears threatening to fall. "Don't you dare shed another tear for that man!" Armani demanded. "You are smart and beautiful, but he lost you and it's his loss! You have already shed enough tears behind him, so do not shed a single tear! If you do Mia, I promise you will have to find your own way home," Armani said through clenched teeth. All of a sudden, her face softened as she reached in her purse to hand me some tissue. I quickly wiped my eyes and looked in the nearest car's side mirror to check my face. Still perfect. I swallowed the huge lump that was still in my throat and did a light jog to catch up with Armani. Yes, the bitch got me together, gave me tissue, and left me standing there.

By the time I caught up with Armani, she had done already passed through the food court and was heading in the direction of *Ardene.* That store sells jewelry, hats, scarves, sunglasses, pretty much any accessory you can think of. It's not necessarily in my price range, so I decide against following her.

The mall isn't really the place for me because I'm more of a behind the scenes type of person. If there is a smaller store I can run in and grab something cute and cheap, I'd much rather go there. It's always too many people at the mall, not to mention, I don't like being bothered. See, I'm one of those really friendly people that hate people, if that makes sense. For instance, if we are all sitting around talking, I can most definitely work the crowd and become the life of the party. It's like I have an alluring spirit. Now, at the same time, if I have the option to stay at home versus going to a party, you will more than likely find me sitting on my couch watching Netflix. It's just how I am.

"Tamia?" I hear a voice call out to me as I scroll through the mall alone. I'm now near *Aeropostale,* so I head in to check out their crop top selections. "Tamia," I hear again. This time, I decide to answer. As soon as I turn around, I'm face to face with Lisa Cunningham. There is no secret that I don't care for her at all. I would say I hate her but I'd have to actually care about her at one point to hate her, and I just can't say that I have.

"What are you doing here?" she asks.

"Why?" I ask, taking her in. She is the complete opposite of me: dark as night, really slim, short hair, and a Marilyn Monroe mole in the exact same spot as Marilyn.

"Just curious," she pauses. "Didn't know you lived here, is all."

"Well, I do," I respond, turning around to finish browsing.

"Well, in case you were wondering, Amere is here as well. We live together. Just moved here last week with our daughter, Amiria," she says with a smirk.

I refuse to let this bitch see me cry. Fuck their whole family! "Do you want a cookie?" I ask because I'm trying to figure out why she would, damn near chase me down into a store, just tell me that they moved here and they all live together. Who the fuck cares? Well, I kind of do, but I'll never let her know that.

"Lisa? Baby, where are you?" I hear an all too familiar voice call out. I look at Lisa, who is still standing in front of me with this stupid smirk on her face.

Amere

Man, I have no fucking clue why Lisa's ass wanted to move to Detroit. I met her back on the coast. She was originally a fling. Just some easy pussy to get, and I was for damn sure taking full advantage of getting it! The only thing was, I already had a good girl.

Tamia was ever nigga's dream. She cooked, cleaned, she's smart, beautiful, amazing body, good conversation, don't club, and no kids. Need I say more? Shawty was perfect but Lisa was every nigga's fantasy! She was always willing to fuck and if it was that time of the month, she would just suck a couple of nuts out of me. See, Tamia was a virgin when I met her and it took me a little over a year to get it. After I got it, she was supposed to go wild for the dick, like most females do once they get that cherry popped. You know how y'all go dumb over the dick! Tamia didn't, her ass was still focused on school and working. I was always her last thought but with Lisa, I was her every thought. Dating them both gave me the best of both worlds. I could lay up and fuck Lisa all day while Tamia was at school or working, and then go home and Tamia would have my plate in the microwave and she would be asleep. Tamia never asked me what I did all day or who I was with. She never questioned anything. She was always too focused on her damn self to give a damn about me and what I was doing. That's why, when I fucked up and got Lisa pregnant, I ain't try to hide it.

Lisa and Tamia knew each other from school but ran in different circles, so I never had to worry about the two clashing. Tamia was quiet back then and only ran with Armani, while Lisa was friends with every damn body and went out more than I did. Anyway, when Lisa told me she was pregnant, I didn't give a damn about Tamia's feelings. Hell, Tamia didn't even find out through me. She wasn't on any social media sites but Armani was. Well, Armani and Lisa are Facebook friends, and Lisa posted a picture of her sonogram and tagged me saying welcome to fatherhood. Long story short, Armani told Tamia and she was done with me, just like that. She didn't snap on a nigga or nothing, so I knew her ass didn't care about me to begin with. What bitch just dumps her dude because she heard he got a baby on the way without at least snapping?

Two months after she cut me off completely, I mean cut all ties, I realized how much I really love her ass! I wish she would have let me explain my side of things, then maybe, we could have worked it out. I tried texting her but I kept getting an automatic message saying my text couldn't be delivered. It wasn't until I called her that I realized she had gotten that phone cut off. I went by our old place and she had moved out, but there was a letter on the door in her handwriting.

Dear Amere,
I loved you. You hurt me. I'm done.
No Longer Yours,
Tamia

I read that letter over and over, hoping the words would change. I needed her like I needed oxygen to breathe and she left me over one fucking mistake! I was so mad. I drove to Armani's house because I needed her help. I went over Armani's house every day for three weeks before she let me in. It was something different about Armani, but I couldn't quite place it. Anyway, when I tried that next week, Armani was gone as well.

Since Tamia left me, I decided to do what's considered right and be with Lisa for the baby. We ended up having a daughter that Lisa named Amiria. Then all of a sudden, Lisa decides we need new scenery and what better place to start over than Detroit? So, here we are.

I done let Lisa drag me to this big ass mall after we dropped Amiria off with Lisa's cousin, Kylie. Anyway, before I can get the car parked good, Lisa is out the car and heading into the mall. Stupid bitch! I can't stand her, for real y'all. I'm only there because Amiria needs a mother and father in one household. That and if I leave, I know I won't be able to be with my baby girl everyday anymore. Lisa can't cook shit, not even scrambled eggs! Hell, she fixed me a bowl of cereal one day and had too much milk in it! She doesn't clean right. She just straightens up and don't get me started on laundry! I have to do it because every time she does it, our clothes end up a different color! Now she done convinced me we need new furniture, so we're heading to the furniture store in *Devonshire Mall*.

When I find the furniture store, I can't find Lisa's ass nowhere in it, so I walk through the mall yelling her name like she's my fucking child.

"Lisa baby. Where are you?" I yell because I know she's close; I can smell her Paris Hilton perfume. She doesn't know it but since that was the only thing I had left from Tamia, I started making Lisa wear it, so she reminded me somewhat of her.

"Li-" My eyes gotta be playing tricks on me. There is no way in hell I'm standing here looking at my heart talking to my baby mama. Alright well, my girlfriend but damn, being my girl doesn't compare to having my heart. Lisa could never have all of me because Tamia still has my heart.

"Tee? W-wh-what are you doing here?" I stammer. I can't believe we are face to face! It's been four years since I've seen her and time has definitely been on her side. She is even more beautiful than I remembered, her hair is longer, and her body is more toned, like she works out religiously. But, she still looks feminine and soft. Tamia is still the baddest female I've ever seen.

"Shopping," she responds dryly as she turns to continue what she was doing probably before Lisa's ass followed her in here. See, I know Lisa followed her because Lisa doesn't shop in *Aeropostale*. It's one of the stores on her *broke people store* list, so I already know what happened. I can only imagine what was said though. From the look on Tamia's face, she doesn't look bothered at all, which further proves my point that she never cared about a nigga.

"Not *here* as in this store, Tee. Here as in Detroit," I say, walking up to her.
"Well, if you must know, Armani and I moved here for school. I run track at UMA while I'm studying to become a Healthcare Administrator," she says with determination. I can tell she's been doing good and I almost don't want to get at her, but shit, what's a man to do when he can't move on?

"I looked for you. I-"

"Don't!" She interrupted me with anger in her eyes. I know this look all too well. Tamia's short black ass will pop off at the drop of a dime and it doesn't matter where you are or who you are. I've seen her do it. I take a step back with my hands up.

"I'm sorry Tee," I try apologizing but she brushes past me out of the store, running dead into some dude with dreads.

"I'm sorry beautiful. Excuse me. I wasn't watching where I was going." He apologized like it was his fault when she clearly was the one who ran into him trying to get away from me.

I watched as she looked up at him before rolling her eyes, telling him fuck off before she walked away. He just stood there watching her before shaking his head walking away. It wasn't until Lisa cleared her throat that I remembered she was right there. I looked over at her and she was mean mugging me with her arms folded, like my reunion with Tamia wasn't her damn fault! Had she not followed her in a store, I wouldn't have been looking for her and ran into Tamia at the same time. So, everything that she witnessed was her own damn doing.

"Let's go!" I say pissed off because once again, Tamia didn't give me a chance to explain myself! I swear, she's so fucking selfish sometimes!

"But we haven't even gone to the furniture store yet," Lisa pleaded.

"Well, had you gone to the furniture store instead of following my girl in here, we would have furniture!" I snapped. It wasn't until Lisa slapped the shit out of me that I realized I called Tamia my girl.

"I'm your girl and the mother of your child, and you will respect me as both!" she says before storming off. I watched her walk out of the store and didn't even bother to chase her. Shit, I gotta figure out how to get my girl back, keep my family together, and get my money up!

I had just started making a come up back on the coast when Lisa's dumb ass decided she needed a new change of scenery, and she was taking my daughter, so I had to follow suit. I think I know now why she chose Detroit, out of all the places in the world to move too.

Anyway, we've only been here a week and nobody seems to know who the boss is around here, so I can get on. Seems like I'm fucked but when there's a will, then there's a way. I will get my girl back, I will keep my family, and I will be the next King of Detroit! Being the king will be the easiest because they don't have one right now.

Armani

I promise, sometimes I don't know how I can deal with Tamia! She's so weak minded! Can you believe when she saw Amere, she was about to fucking cry? Like real fucking tears! This nigga cheated their whole relationship and Tamia was blind to it all until I showed her the sonogram Lisa's maggot ass posted on Facebook. After that, she didn't even want to face him. Neither of them got the closure they needed, which is why a few months after they broke up, he came knocking on my door.

Yeah, he came banging on my door like the police two nights after I killed Steve, so can you imagine how I was acting when I opened the door? Shit, had he been the police, I would have been arrested on the spot for standing there fidgeting like a damn fiend! Anyway, it took a few weeks before I actually allowed him to enter, and it was only because I knew Tamia was already in Detroit at orientation for school. We talked and chilled for a few hours that day. For some reason, unknown to mankind, he placed total blame on Tamia. This nigga literally called her perfect and selfish in one breath! Like seriously? I wanted to say, really nigga?

Anyway, I had to give this bitch a quick pep talk because her ass was always running from her problems! You can't run from your problems, baby and I'm here to let you know that! You have to face everything life throws you head on. When life throws you lemons, throw them bitches right back! So, after I broke it down so it can forever be broken for Tamia, I handed her some Kleenex out of my purse and walked away. She's a real silly bitch if she thought I was going to remain a guest to her pity party.

I walked through the food court and remembered I needed a new scarf, so I decided to go to *Ardene's* first. So, I'm walking through the food court and I see this fine ass dark skinned dude! Babee, this nigga had dreads that were neatly done and pulled back into a ponytail. He had on all black Levi jeans with a crisp black T-shirt. I couldn't see his shoes from where I'm standing but he was low riding and his boxers were black too. He glanced in my direction, like he could sense me staring a hole through his sexy ass, but then he kept walking.

Now you know your girl bugging right now because I know I'm the shit and ain't nan nigga ever caught a glimpse and didn't want a sample! Who the fuck dude think he is? I watch him from a distance, making sure to keep at least four stores in between us and whenever I think he's going to look back, I look into a store. So, I'm following him for a good ten minutes before he goes into *Children's Place*. Fuck, this nigga got children! I can't do a nigga with kids unless he's strictly my sponsor, but I had hopes for sexy chocolate.

I turn around so I can head back and get my scarf. After I purchase it and walk out of the store, I see Lisa's skinny ass walk into *Aeropostale*. I'm on high alert because I know Tamia loves that store. I figure if she ain't already in there, she will be soon and I didn't want her to have to face Lisa alone! The closer I get to the store, the more I can tell that I'm a little too late. Since neither of them knows I'm near, I'm just going to watch the exchange.

I'm slick pissed that Tamia ruined my day of shopping with her little sensitive ass but at least she finally gets to get hers! I know you're thinking, only a trifling bitch would want their best friend to get anything negative, but you don't understand! I love Tamia, I really do but nothing ever comes hard for her. She gets everything she wants and never has to work hard for anything. She wasn't the one being raped all those nights by Steve, but she was able to track him down, so we could kill him. Tamia isn't the one that wanted to go to school and become a nurse, but she got a track scholarship and she's only a few months away from getting her Bachelor's in Healthcare Administration! It's not fair because I didn't even get fucking accepted into the school!

Tamia has it all, so she'll never understand how I feel about everything. I'm honestly just tired of her always getting what she wants. I applaud Lisa for raining on Tamia's parade because I'm not able to!

I watch as the two go back and forth a few minutes, and Tamia is handling herself well! You would have never thought that she was about to cry when she first saw them from the parking lot. Anyway, I watch Tamia turn her back on Lisa, and I can only hope that Lisa hits her, so I can run up on that ass and give her 100 hands!

Not even a full minute later, we all hear Amere calling Lisa and the look on Tamia's face is priceless! She wipes it away so fast and I gotta admit, the bitch is good. I didn't get pissed off until he started talking to Tamia, like his damn girlfriend wasn't standing there! They were having a full blown conversation like it was just the two of them. All I could think of was it couldn't be me.

I smelled Gucci Cologne and when I looked up, I saw sexy chocolate just standing there texting on his phone, completely oblivious to what's taking place a few feet away. I check myself out in the mirror on the wall but before I can approach him, Tamia's crybaby ass storms past me and runs right into sexy.

Now, I just knew he was gone curse her from here back to the coast, but he apologized! I couldn't fucking believe it! I wanted to yell, NIGGA YOU WEREN'T EVEN IN MOTION!!! The fuck is he sorry for? Tamia told that nigga to fuck off and kept going. I swear, she's such a drama queen. This bitch does the most.

I turn back to look at Lisa, and Amere and this bitch is just staring at the back of his head when she should be hitting him in it for disrespecting her like that. As if completely ignoring her while he talked to his ex-girlfriend wasn't enough, this nigga calls Tamia his girl! Like present tense, girl! Like, he's currently in a relationship with Tamia, and Lisa slaps the dog shit out of this dog ass nigga! Then she snaps on him and storms out! Man, these bitches storm off game is so strong. Shaking my head. I guess I'll go find Tamia.

When I find Tamia, she's outside on the truck, looking crazy. "What's wrong with you?" I ask like I don't already know.

"Girl, wait til I tell you about it," she responds. Well, come on and let's go to the food court and talk.

She reluctantly hopped down and walked back inside of the mall with me. We both decided on fried rice and general chicken to eat for lunch. "So, what happened?" I asked because she's clearly not going to talk about it on her own. I want to see if she will be one hundred about the situation.

"So, I'm in Aero looking for crop tops when Lisa walks in!" she exclaimed.

"Nooo!" I said.

"Bitch yes, so she walks up to me and is basically telling me that her, Amere and their daughter, Amiria, just moved down here sometime last week. I guess she just wanted me to know," she said, which was news to me. I couldn't exactly hear everything that was being said, but I guess I missed out on hearing her lie.

"I just asked her if she wanted a cookie, then Amere walks in, calling her baby and shit!" she said honestly, and I'm mad because that's yet another good thing people will say about their precious Tamia.

"What happened when he came in?" I asked.

"Nothing really, he tried to apologize for how things ended with us, but I didn't want to hear it, especially when he's standing in front of me with his new bitch and they have a whole family," she says then takes a deep breath, like she just used all of her wind.

"Wow!" was all I could say. I wanted to mention dude, but I couldn't without letting her know that I had witnessed the entire altercation and did nothing to help.

"So, I ran out of the store and ran into Rashard!" she said smiling.

"Rashard? Who is he?" I asked, really wanting to know. At least I now have a name to go with his sexy chocolate body.

"This football player at UMA. He tried to talk to me yesterday before my track meet. Well, afterwards too, but I told him to fuck off," she said while laughing.

Now I'm looking at this bitch with the, *I just ate shit face,* you know the face Kevin Hart was talking about. She has got to be the dumbest chick on the planet to pass all that chocolate goodness up! She probably thinks she's better than him. "What's funny?" I ask because I missed the joke. Hell, I wanted him and here her simple ass is giving him a hard time because like I said before; she never has to work for anything.

"Nothing really. Just that when I ran into him today, I told him to fuck off again," she said.

"You're so lame, Mia," I stated dryly, before getting up to throw my plate away. I didn't even wait for her to follow suit before I headed out the door to my truck.

Rashard

After I left *Dead Man's Zone,* I drove to one of my condos to shit, shave, and shower. I jumped fresh and headed down to the mall. I forgot to call and make sure Michelle would fit me in to get my dreads retwisted tomorrow, so I grab my cell phone to call her. It went straight to voicemail, so I just sat my phone in the cup holder.

Ding. My phone chimed, indicating I had a text message.

"Who texted me?" I asked my car. See, whenever I got in my car, I would connect my phone to it, so I wouldn't have to text and drive or hold the phone to talk. It's completely hands free.

"Chardae," the animated voice replied.

"What did she say?" I asked.

"Are you coming over?" the animated voice replied.

"Reply no, I'm good," I said to my car. Once I heard a bell, I knew my message had been sent.

See, Chardae would be a good catch for someone who had the patience to get her ass right, that guy just ain't me. How can I get her right when I'm not right my damn self? I mean, I do have a lot going on but I need my woman to have vision, so she can help get me on the right path. See, I'm in school and playing ball, but that's not what I want to do. What I really want to do is make it so when I have kids, they won't have to work. I don't want my career to be something I could get hurt in, which is why I'm not trying to go pro, but I'm not trying to stay in the drug game. In three months, I'll be graduating with my Bachelors in Business Management. My only problem is I have no interest, as far as what type of business to start.

So anyway, speaking of drug game, it's some cat from out of town going around trying to get put on. I've had several runners come up to me this last week telling me how hungry dude is. To avoid him being an enemy, I'm going to have to come up with a spot for him on my team. I have to meet with him first, so I can fill him out.

Thirty minutes later, I pull up to the mall and circle the entire parking lot three times. I always do this to see if I recognize any cars, to see if anything stands out like someone just sitting idle or whatever. I always have to watch my back because you never know who's lurking.

I park and get out with no destination in mind, just kind of window shopping I guess you can say. All of a sudden, the hairs on the back of my neck stand up and I have that feeling that someone's watching me. I take my time scanning the crowd in front of me before I turn around and make eye contact with this light skinned beauty! I mean, this chick got it! Big titties, big ass, and her hair stands out to me because of the bright red tips. Something about her gives me this eerie feeling though, so I turn around and keep walking.

Now, I'm just randomly walking, so imagine my surprise when I get that feeling again! Instead of turning around, I look at the glass surrounding each store, so I can see her reflection. The bitch is without a doubt bad ass fuck, but why is she following me? My thoughts go back to what Smurf said about it being a bad bitch that robbed them and I'm thinking it could have been her.

I slowly and inconspicuously remove my .45 and attach my silencer before looking back. I noticed every time I would turn my head slightly; she would act like something caught her attention in the store. She was slick but I'm slicker.

Now I'm looking in each store trying to see who has the least amount of people in it. *Children's Place* is damn near empty! Perfect! The only person in there is the store clerk, and I can just shoot them both and walk out like nothing happened. I turn into the store and start going through the nearest clothing rack as I watch her simultaneously. She frowns before turning to walk away.

I don't know if I'm just being paranoid and she just wanted to holla or not, but you can never be too careful. I walk right back out of the store and follow her to *Ardene's*, and watch as she browsed around and buys a damn scarf! Why yall bitches be buying scarves? It ain't that fucking cold. Then that little thin ass scarf she bought wouldn't help her here anyway. Once I realize she was a thirsty bitch and not an actual threat, I walk right back out the store to continue my stroll.

Ding. My text message tone goes off.

Chardae: come by

Rashard: No!

Chardae: we need to talk

Rashard: about?

Chardae: I'm pregnant

My heart skipped a beat and I became frozen in place. All of a sudden, I was damn near knocked over. I got so pissed off, I almost hit her but I saw who it was. It was the beauty from the track meet, Tamia. Man, this chick is gorgeous and she doesn't even try to be. I don't think she knows how good she looks.

"I'm sorry, beautiful. Excuse me. I wasn't watching where I was going," I said to her, even though I knew I wasn't moving when she ran into me. She looked into my eyes and for a quick second, nothing and nobody else mattered.

"Fuck off!" she said and kept going. I couldn't help but to chuckle a little bit because shawty is going to be a handful. That's why I have two, so I can handle her. I don't usually go for bitches with attitudes but it's something about Tamia that got ya boy gone! I don't know what it is because the only thing I know about her is she runs track. I watch her until I can't see her anymore and from the corner of my eye, I can see the chick that was following me earlier, crouched down behind a clothing rack.

I don't think anyone else has seen her but I need to figure out who she is. I exited out of Chardae's dumb ass text message and switched to camera mode, so I can take her picture. I'm going to figure out who this chick is if it's the last thing I do. I also noticed a couple inside the store arguing and ole girl hung around watching them, so

I can only assume that they having some type of lover's quarrel as I walk away.

Since I don't have anything to do, I head to *Carte Blanche* to see if Michelle is at work and holla at my boy Raphael. Nobody knows but Raphael isn't the sole owner of *Carte Blanche*. I own 70% of the club, which is why it's decked out the way it is. I have everything placed the way I need things to be, in case things ever go south. Let's say the Feds come in and I'm in one of the VIP booths, well there are two secret elevators. One of them, only certain dancers, Raphael, and I know about. The other is located on a secret sub floor that only Raphael and I know about.

One thing about me you will figure out if you haven't already is I stay prepared for anything. Any time you think someone has one up on me, remember, I'm always two steps ahead, even when it doesn't seem like it.

Anyway, I pulled around back to my designated parking spot and entered my code into the digital pad that appears only when my car is parked in this specific spot. I got my man, Dave, to come install some type of electronic equipment, so the pad would somehow be able to tell it's my car and knows when to extend the digital pad. Dave told me something about my tire tread, length and width of the car is what makes this work. This is why I have custom tires.

Once I enter my code, my tires are locked into place and the parking spot lowers, going underground and within minutes, my tires are unlocked, so I can drive off. I always look in my rearview mirror to make sure my parking spot goes back up securely before driving off. See, the club has an underground parking lot where I keep all of my vehicles. I only drive my Honda around town, my luxury whips are for traveling. I have six different parking spots that lower into the ground for underground parking, so that's six different exits if the Feds come in.

I hop out of my car, walking to the elevator that only I know about. This is the only elevator that you can't tell is an elevator with the naked eye. The other two secret elevators have a small ignition that's barely noticeable on the right side, and only Raphael, Candy, and I can get you on and off. This particular elevator doesn't have one. I walk to it and place both hands against the wall that is actually the elevator door. A small slot that's eye level opens, scanning both eyes in less than ten seconds before the full elevator door opens.

This elevator goes directly to my office, which sits in the middle of the ceiling, so I can see everyone and everything. I have cameras installed for the things I miss and I view them every single day, most days from home. No one knows how to get to my office or even where exactly in the building it is because I can see through it, but looking up from the floor, it simply looks like a ceiling. It's also bulletproof, in case someone decides to come in the club shooting up the place.

I sit down behind my huge black, cherry oak wood desk and decided to watch the monitors. I can see on the very first monitor that something isn't right. There is a guy posted in each corner. I can see that one of them has his eyes trained on the VIP booths, another one is following Candy with his eyes, the third one is watching Raphael talk to Brittany, the bartender, and the fourth is watching the door.

I sat there watching them for ten minutes before I noticed the resemblance between Brittany and the guy watching Candy. I immediately grabbed my pager and sent 911 to Raphael. I watch him silence it without checking to see what it said, even though I specifically told this man that we will only use these pagers in case of an emergency like this one! His ass in the middle of a war zone and don't know he's being played! Brittany and Michelle have both been trying hard to get promotions, but neither of them fit my qualifications for the jobs they wanted. Therefore, whenever Raphael came to me with it, I always told him it was a no go.

Anyway, since Raphael didn't check the pager, I hit him on his cell.

"What's up Casper?" Raphael answered his phone. I immediately got pissed because this dude seriously ignored the pager because he was talking to Brittany! I have told him time and time again not to fraternize with his employees, but he always throws Michelle in my face. I know you're thinking he's right, but Michelle has no clue I'm her boss.

"Cut the bull nigga and peep your surroundings!" I scream at him, trying not to say too much over the phone. I'm watching him look around all suspicious and shit, and he gone let them fools know he's on to them. I quickly page Candy 911, and watch as she discreetly pulls her pager out and walk swiftly to Raphael's office. When I see the light outside his office turn green, I know the lines are now secure.

"Man, ion see nothing," Raphael groans.

"Hold on a sec, bruh," I say, clicking Candy on the line with us.

"What's going on boss?" Candy asks, as soon as she hears the click. See, Candy is the only person other than Raphael that knows who owns the greatest percentage of this club. She also knows not to say anything to anyone.

"Peep this, don't interrupt me. If you have any questions, wait until I'm done talking," I tell them.

"Cool," they reply in unison.

"Raph, I want you to lean against the bar. Use the Bluetooth, so no one knows you're still on the phone. Candy, look under Raph's desk and get the .45 and its silencer out, and place in your garter belt. Look in his closet and grab the black tennis skirt to hide it." I give them directions quickly and watch the monitors. I can see them doing as they're told. I zoom in on the guys, noticing they are now exchanging glances. Some shit is about to pop off and I have no idea what. I can't find Brittany on any of the monitors, so I know she done got her ass out of dodge.

"Raph, there is a guy in every corner of the club. One of them is watching the VIP booths, the second is waiting on you to come out of the office, Candy, so stay put until I say go. The third one is watching you Raph and the fourth in the far right corner is watching the door. Raph, look at the second one without him noticing and tell me who he looks like to you," I tell my people as I look through my arsenal closet.

It's times like these that make me glad I put these cameras all over the place. I quickly check my surveillance cameras that are outside. "BINGO!" I say out loud to myself because I found Brittany. She's standing outside next to an all-black Tahoe truck. After looking around the club parking lot, I see there are four other all black Tahoe trucks scattered all over the parking lot. I can't tell how many are occupying each vehicle because the windows are tinted darkly.

I grab my phone and call Dre. He picks up on the third ring. "What's good Shard?" he says, answering his phone.

"Not shit right now, bruh. Check this, I need you and Twan to grab your whole team and get down to *Carte Blanche* like yesterday," I say into the phone.

"Iight bet" he says, disconnecting the call. See, that's why he's my dude, my right hand!

Next, I call my boy, Tre, and tell him the same thing followed by Deuce, Big B and Trinity.

"Ah, fuck man!" Raphael says into his Bluetooth, once he figures out what I was trying to tell him.

"What?" Candy asks, still in Raphael's office.

"That bitch, Brittany, set us up man. Fuck!" he says.

"Calm down, my nigga," I tell him, once I see the guy that's watching him start paying more attention to his movements than he was a moment ago.

"Don't worry, help is on the way," I tell Raphael and Candy.

"I'm fucking Brittany up when I see her!" Candy said, clearly pissed off. I can't even say shit because I was thinking the same damn thing.

I check the outside monitors again and I can see Dre, Tre, Deuce, Big B, and Trinity, along with their whole team, pull into the parking lot. I breathed a sigh of release. "Let's get this party started," I say to myself.

Tamia

I cannot believe the nerve of this bitch Lisa or her nigga, Amere, to come at me that way in the mall. Lisa definitely has some nerve, approaching me to begin with on the bullshit! Yes, she was his side chick while we were together, but she did not take him from me. Don't ever get it twisted, baby. Let the record show, I left his dog ass after I found about her pregnancy. Our whole relationship, I knew he was doing his thing. Fact of the matter is I loved him and I didn't care. My main focus was finishing school, so I can better myself. I've never had time to compete with the next bitch because truth of the matter is, the only person I'm trying to be better than is the person I was yesterday.

Anyway, I never said anything to him because he was home every night, he never stayed out late, and most importantly, he never brought home any STDs. We didn't have sex much because I didn't like it. I hardly ever came, so any chance I could play sleep, you better believe I did. That's how I knew he was in the streets doing his own thing. Let me take the lie back about never cumming because I did, every once in a while but if I didn't get mine before he got his, then I just wouldn't get it.

Armani kept telling me to leave him alone but I never would listen to her. She didn't understand because she never had a love like ours. I was the perfect girlfriend! Well, nobody's perfect but minus our damn near nonexistent sex life, everything was perfect. I cooked breakfast and dinner every single day. I washed and ironed all of our clothes and kept our apartment clean. We had been living together from the time I was sixteen until I was eighteen. I've been emancipated since I was thirteen though, and I already had that apartment, so he moved in with me.

It wasn't until Armani showed me Lisa's sonogram on Facebook that I had had finally seen Amere for the dog ass nigga he was! I was so pissed; I moved out of my own damn apartment! After Armani and I killed Steve, her mom turned to drugs to cope, so she was never home and I basically moved in with her. I packed my stuff up and moved without saying anything to him. Well, except the simple, short and sweet note I left him taped on the front door.

Armani called me everything under the sun for not confronting them both but that ain't never been me. You will never be able to fix your mouth to say Tamia was fighting over anybody. I don't care enough about anyone to go start some shit to keep him. No, fuck that! Its way easier to say fuck him and keep it moving. I'm not on Facebook or anything else, so it's not like I would have to see them together. Now, these bitches want to move where I ran off to, to get away from them! I'm not running this time! I have three months left before I graduate and Detroit is home now, so I'm here to stay.

The way she approached me was like she knew something I didn't. She had this stupid looking smirk on her face the whole time we were talking. Well, until Amere's sexy, light skin ass walked up with all those yummy tattoos! The level of disrespect was at an all-time high when this nigga started apologizing for his child! I kept glancing at Lisa and that smirk was long gone! Ha! That's what her ass get for cornering me.

When I ran out of the store, I ran dead into Rashard. I got the weirdest feeling when I looked into his eyes. It was almost as if no one else was there but I can't have that feeling! Nooo, buddy! Nobody will get the chance to hurt me like Amere did! No sir! I'm too focused on Tamia to focus on anything else. I'm twenty-two and about to graduate with my Bachelor's in Health Administration! I have no kids and as soon as I get a job, Armani will be living there alone because I'm tired of cleaning up after her.

Anyway, I told Rashard to fuck off and ran to the truck. I didn't realize that I didn't have the keys until I got out there, so I just leaned on it waiting on Armani. It wasn't long before Armani came sashaying out of the mall with a serious mug on her face. I swear, lately, we have been bumping heads a lot! It's like she really doesn't like me, but she tolerates me. For what reason, I don't know. She asked what was wrong and we went inside the food court, so I could give her a brief rundown of what happened.

Before the conversation was completely over, she got up and walked away. She didn't even wait for me to get up! Hell, I had done most of the talking, so I wasn't done eating yet. I closed my plate and followed behind her confused. I don't understand what I said that ticked her off but like I said before, I'm not about to argue with her while she's driving. The whole ride home was a silent one. I kept stealing glances, trying to figure out what her problem is with me but I decided to say fuck it!

I'm a grown kind of person. What I mean by that is if I have a problem with you, you won't have to wonder about it because it will be addressed. I don't have time to worry about her when I have two exams on Monday. As soon as we pulled up, I hopped out and went into my room, closing the door behind me to get some studying done. I love Armani to death, but I'm not about to kiss her ass! She has known me long enough to know that.

By the time I finished studying, it was 12:30 and I was starving! I remembered I took some chicken wings out earlier, so I decided to fry them and make some mac and cheese. As soon as I opened my room door, I could hear Armani screaming and moaning like nobody's business. I walked down the hall in the dark and fell, tripping over a really dark colored Timberland boot. The light was off and I couldn't see exactly what color.

Being pissed was an understatement because I had to clean up this nigga's clothes again! I folded them up and sat everything outside of her room door. When I walked in the kitchen, I wasn't surprised to see dishes in the sink, since my roommate never cleans up after herself. I turn the fryer on to warm the grease up before I started cleaning the kitchen.

By the time I finished cooking and fixing my plate, Armani and her guy were done smashing. Hopefully, after I ate, I could sleep peacefully. So, I'm sitting in the living room watching *Revenge* on Netflix while I'm eating my food.

"Oh shit!" I hear a male voice in the hall. I turn to look but in the dark, all I can see is him running back into Armani's room. I guess I must have spooked him. Now, instead of moans, all I can hear is them arguing. Armani must have turned some music on to drown their voices out but I can still hear them; I just can't make out what they are saying. After I finish eating, I cut the tv off and go into the kitchen to wash my plate. I don't hear them arguing anymore, so I guess they have gone to sleep.

I go in my room and put all my books up before I lay down to get some rest. About ten minutes later, I hear my door open and I look up to see Armani standing there, glaring down at me. Not knowing what her problem is and not being willing to take a chance, I hop out of the bed.

"What the hell you doing, Mia?" she asked, with a now confused look on her face.

"Well shit, you act like I said something to piss you off earlier and you haven't talked to me since. Now, you in my room, mugging me from the door!" I respond, frowning. She laughs. Not a chuckle but a deep hearty laugh! So now, I'm looking at her confused.

"You did piss me off earlier, but I wasn't talking to you because you weren't talking to me. I came in here mugging you because I smelled that fried chicken, but you ain't save me none, helfa!" she said still laughing.

I sat down on my bed taking it all in. I still didn't believe her, and the fact that I know she isn't keeping it a buck with me is making me not trust her anymore. "Well, I guess I'll let you go on back to sleep," she says, locking my door then closing it. Not long after that, I heard the front door open and close, then her shower came on. I guess she let her sponsor out and now, she's in the shower.

The next morning, I'm up at 7am cooking eggs, grits, bacon, and pancakes. I hate eating late because for some reason, I always wake up starving! I have a track meet today at one, so I shouldn't have any cramps or anything.

"Good morning, beautiful," I hear from the hallway. When I turn to see who it is, it's the sponsor that caught me pleasuring myself a few days ago. My face flushes immediately, thinking about what I did as I drop the spatula.

"You don't have to be nervous around me, sweetie. You weren't nervous the other day," he says with a smile. I reached down to grab the spatula and started cleaning it without responding to him. "So, why don't you let me take you out some time, miss? It will be my pleasure," he continues.

"No thank you. Have a good day," I say as I finish fixing my plate and head into my room. I was going to eat in the living room but not with Armani's sponsor hitting on me!

Armani

After listening to Tamia recant the events, my stomach took a turn for the worse. I was disgusted! I mean, who does she think she is? It's not like she's God's greatest gift to man! I bet if I told her how I felt, she would have one excuse after another backing up each thing she has done wrong to me! Ok well, she hasn't actually done anything wrong to me per se, but why do she have to be good at everything? Why doesn't she have to work for anything? Shit ain't fair! I worked my butt off after Steve's no good ass raped me to keep my grades up high enough to get into school. My problem was I didn't have any guidance!

My mother was a "ain't shit ass bitch" that let her boyfriend rape her only daughter! Her only fucking child! Then she wanted to turn around and pretend like she gave a damn! The bitch cared more about Steve "leaving her" than she did me and before I knew it, she was cracked out! I remember my first time catching her like it was yesterday.

Tamia and I decided to catch the public transportation bus home instead of walking, like we normally did. "I can't wait to go off to school!" Tamia said. "Girl, you and me both! What are you going for?" I replied. "I don't know. I'll figure it out eventually though. I may just go and take the basic classes until I decide what I want to do. What are you going for?" she asked. "Girl, I'm going to be the best registered nurse anyone has ever seen! I'm not going to have any kids, so I can be a traveling nurse!" I said excitedly. "That's whats up, Mani! I'll be there for you every step of the way. I'm glad you didn't let what happened to you stop you," she said. "I know, me too," I replied somberly.

The bus stopped, allowing us to get off at our stop. Riding the bus cut our time in half and then some! I noticed Tamia wasn't talking anymore as we turned on my street, but I didn't know what to say. Unlike Tamia, I never knew how to comfort anyone. Hell, I can't even comfort myself!

"Hey, I'm going to head on to my apartment. Do you want to come over?" Tamia asked. "Naw, I'm tired," I replied but I really wanted to tell her what had been going on. My mom had been acting strange and I needed to make sure she was ok before I did anything else. Had I known what I know now, I would have walked over to Tamia's apartment with her.

As always, the door was unlocked but I was not prepared for what I saw next. My mother sat on the floor Indian style in front of the couch, inhaling deeply while sucking on a crack pipe. Next to her was a soda can with a hole in it and a straw, like she tried and failed miserably at making a homemade pipe. I cleared my throat to make my presence known but she just started rocking. I stood there watching my mother smile and rock before she closed her eyes, leaning back against the couch.

I walked up to her, shaking her shoulder roughly. "MOM! WHAT THE HELL IS WRONG WITH YOU?!" I yelled before smacking the pipe out of her hand. She jumped up and hit me so fast, I didn't have time to react. I stood there staring her down as she breathed hard, staring right back at me. She walked away heading in the direction of the now, broken crack pipe. When she saw it was broken, she started screaming like a maniac and ran towards me, screaming and swinging on me. I tried holding her down but the drugs had her so strong. I wanted to fight her back but this is my mom, and I couldn't bring myself to do it.

"Why did you do that?" she screamed. "You keep taking everything from me! I hate you! You've ruined my life! I should've had a damn abortion; you piece of shit! Why would you take the only thing I had left that made me happy?!" she continued screaming and by now she's slobbering, and I'm trying to fight back my tears.

I turned to walk away from her, only for her to start back fighting me. I lightly pushed her onto the couch so I could go to my room but she jumped right back up, tripping and hitting her head on the table. I looked back because she wasn't screaming anymore. I walked closer to her and when I saw her chest rising and falling, I knew she had only knocked herself, so I went back into my room. I vowed never to fall in love and never have children because I didn't want this cycle to continue.

The next morning, I was awakened by a bird outside of my window and searched all over the house for my mom. Needless to say, I couldn't find her and I have only seen her four times since then.

Tamia doesn't know how good she had it, getting emancipated. I was stuck in that house, pretending my mom was at work. Meanwhile, all Tamia had to do was keep a clean house. She will never know my struggle! I drove my truck all the way back to our place in deep thought. I desperately needed to figure out my next move because living with Tamia was causing me to hate her.

As soon as we made it home, she hopped out before I could even park good. I guess she's mad at me but the feeling is mutual! I have my sponsors but I have to do so much to keep them, meanwhile, she got niggas wanting to be with her and she ain't doing shit! Yeah, I'm pissed because we are both some bad bitches, but what makes her better than me? She has no man and I have four. I'm mad because three of them are married and the other one doesn't want anyone to know that he's dealing with me! Now, what kind of shit is that? I never argue or anything, so what makes her better? All she will do is run away at the first sign of trouble!

Ding. My text alert goes off, interrupting my thoughts.

Him: where are you

Armani: home. where are you???

Him: Detroit. Do you live alone

Armani: Yes daddy. Are you coming over?

Him: yea turn your location on so I can find you

A wicked grin spread across my face as my secret sponsor hit me up. He had been talking about moving here to get closer to me, but I thought it was a crock load of shit! Maybe he's ready to finally be with me exclusively. I know he has a girlfriend but if he's here looking for me, then she must mean nothing to him. Well, not much anyway. I quickly hop in the shower to get ready for Daddy. I just got a Brazilian wax Wednesday, so we're good on the shaving part!

Him: I'm outside. lemme in

When I read that message, I got sooo freaking nervous! I quickly walked to Tamia's room and placed my ear to the door. I can hear soft wind and crickets, so I know she's studying. Tamia is weird like that. She cannot focus in silence. She's always saying how silence is far louder than actual noise. That's something I don't understand.

I walk to the door in nothing but a red tank top shirt with a sheer back and black thongs with red thread. When I open the door, Daddy quickly steps in, sucking all over my neck. I moan softly while unbuckling his pants. Once they fall, he kicks his shoes off and one of them land on my pinky toe.

"Ouch!" I yell out, hopping on the other foot. I hop towards my bedroom and when I glance back, he's following close behind, removing his clothes on the way. When we make it completely in the room, I stand on the tips of my toes to get a kiss and like always, he turns his head slightly and I nibble on his neck, like that's what I was going for to begin with.

I roughly push Daddy against the wall and squat down in front of him. Daddy got a big ole dick and you have to know how to work it so you can get yours because I don't think he's that experienced. Sometimes, I wonder why he's such a selfish lover. Either way it goes, I know how to work it, so I have no complaints. When you know your own body, you cum faster because you know which way to rotate your hips and when to rub your clit faster.

I stroked his dick with his balls in my mouth. "You got that first one out the way yet, Daddy?" I ask, looking up at him before taking all of his dick in my mouth. I watch him shake his head no, so I know I need to start working on getting mine now. I reach in between my legs, rubbing my clit with my thumb and fingering myself with my index and middle finger, all the while sucking his dick. When I feel him jerk in my mouth, I pull back and stand to my feet.

"What the fuck, man? I was finna nut!" he said, getting mad.

"I know Daddy, but I needed to feel you first," I replied and watched his frown fade away. See, when you piss a nigga off, you have to stroke his ego to get back into his good graces. I grabbed Daddy's hand and led him to my bed as I climbed up on all fours. He entered me slowly and before I could mention him not putting a condom on first, he was long dicking me! Girl, I started yodeling, the dick was so good! He grabbed my hair, yanking my head back and smacking my ass. I could feel my nut building back up, so I started rubbing my clit faster and faster as he continued to slide in and out of me slowly. He went deeper with each slow thrust. I promise you, if you have never been longed dicked, you need to stop fucking with these short dick niggas! There is nothing like slow, deep, circulating strokes!

"Mmmh Daddy, fuck!" I yelled as I came and he sped up his pace. That was the first time in four years that I came first because he let me, and that was the reassurance I needed to know that he's almost ready. A few minutes later, he came as well and we lay wrapped in each other's arms. Yeah, I think I'm in love.

"What's that smell?" Daddy said, sitting up and rubbing his stomach.

"My roommate must be up cooking. She cooks all the time," I replied.
"Your roommate?" he asked.

"Yea, ain't that what I-" he slapped the shit out of me before I could finish my sentence. That's when I realized that I told him I lived alone! Fuck Tamia! Why would she get up cooking this fucking late!?! Man, I can't stand her ass sometimes!

"I specifically asked you if you had a roommate! Why did you lie?" he asked angrily, but I didn't respond. He hit me so hard, I flew across the room. He walked towards me, and I hopped over the bed and ran to the door. I saw Tamia had done folded up his clothes and sat everything outside my door. I grabbed his clothes and shoes, and brought them inside my room. He snatched his things from me and proceeded to get dressed. I just sat there watching, mad because Tamia knew exactly what she was doing when she got up cooking this damn late!

Daddy didn't say anything else to me as he headed out of here. "Oh Shit!" I heard him say before he ran back into the room.
"Bitch, are you fucking stupid?!" he asked.

"Nigga, I ain't gone be too many more bitches!" I screamed back.

"BITCH! Why the fuck would you lie about having a roommate? What fucking sense do that make?" he asked, walking closer to me. I quickly spit my blade out and got in my fighting stance.

"Like I said, I ain't gone be too many more of your bitches! Ok, I lied about having a roommate, so fucking what! I only lied because I wanted some dick and I knew you wouldn't come over if I told the truth! Why the fuck do I have to be a secret?" I yelled pissed off. "You know what Daddy, don't answer that. Just get the fuck out because I'm done!" I screamed while crying.

His face softened as he approached me. The closer he got, the more I yearned to feel him again. I didn't care about him hitting me or about Tamia getting up ruining a perfectly good moment. All I cared about was Daddy and I in my bed right now. He reached for me and I walked slowly into his embrace. He caressed my face as he stared into my eyes, then slapped the fuck out of me! "Don't you ever lie to me again! And if you ever fix your lips to spit another blade out your mouth like you gone cut me bitch, I'll kill you!" he said through clenched teeth. I looked up at him from the floor with tears streaming down my face. He stayed for another two hours laying across my bed as I sat on the floor crying. Eventually, I cried myself to sleep.

When I realized he was gone, I walked to Tamia's room and opened the door staring at her. Sometimes, I just want to fucking strangle her! I love her too much though. All of a sudden, she jumped up like she was ready to fight. It was almost like she could read my mind.

"What the hell you doing, Mia?" I asked confused because I know I didn't voice any of my thoughts, so this bitch has got to be crazy!

"Well shit, you act like I said something to piss you off earlier and you haven't talked to me since. Now you in my room mugging me from the door!" she responded, frowning at me and ready to throw down. I can't do nothing but laugh! Everything she said makes sense as to why she would be on guard and I'm picturing everything that happened. Can you imagine waking up to someone glaring at you from across the room? Someone you know was pissed off at you. I can, which is why this is all so comical. I'm not a dummy. I know I cannot beat Tamia's ass straight up without my razors, and I already spit it out on Daddy's ass. A lot of good that did me, by the way.

"You did piss me off earlier, but I wasn't talking to you because you weren't talking to me. I came in here mugging you because I smelled that fried chicken, but you ain't save me none helfa!" I said, still laughing. I was really hoping like hell that she bought the excuse I literally just pulled out of my ass. She kept staring at me before she got back in her bed. I saw how she didn't turn her back on me too.

"Well, I guess I'll let you go to sleep," I said to her before locking her door and closing it. I walked slowly to my room, crawling into my bed, and burying myself under the covers before falling back asleep.

I woke up to my text message tone going off. I have it programmed to beep every two minutes after I receive a text until I check it.

Dave: how about breakfast sweetheart?

Armani: Sure. Come over. Its open.

I unlocked the door for Dave and went to take a shower and wash my face. I looked at my reflection as tears slowly streamed down my face. My eyes were puffy and my left cheek was red from Daddy slapping me. I still can't believe he did that to me. I hop in the shower and apply my makeup, making my skin appear flawless. The way I lined my eyes made them look beautiful, instead of puffy. I walked in my closet and decided on my tan romper and gold belt with gold accessories. I normally don't like wearing belts, but this one is wide enough, so you can't see my love handles. It kind of squeezes everything in, making my ass look bigger. As I'm walking down the hall, I can hear Dave and Tamia talking.

"So, why don't you let me take you out some time, Miss? It will be my pleasure." I hear Dave say and my skin begins to boil. I cannot believe he would ask to take me out and before I can even finish getting dressed, he's hitting on Tamia! She can't handle him like I can! The moment she finds out he's married, she will run and move to another country!

"No thank you. Have a good day," she responded like she's too good for him. The nerve of this bitch not to want to date him, like he's beneath her. Well, maybe she said no because she knows he and I are dating. But then again, you never know with Tamia! I'm really starting not to trust her! She's always cooking something just to show off. Hell, she cooked last night in the middle of the night, so I know she's not hungry right now!

"Are you ready to go, Daddy?" I ask, stepping into view and making my presence known.

"Yes, I am. I was just talking to your friend here, but I didn't catch her name," he said, obviously wanting to know her name. She completely ignored us because she was too busy running! She runs from everything, well honestly, everything but a fight. I've known Tamia all of my life, and I've never witnessed or heard of her backing down from a fight. Growing up, she didn't win them all but she fought enough to be A1 like steak sauce with them hands now.

I watched Dave watch Tamia walk down the hall to her bedroom. When he turned back around and caught me staring at him, he didn't even mention or hint at being sorry for being disrespectful. He grabbed my hand and we headed out of the door.
"Where too?" he asked, holding my hand as he drove his yellow Lambo. I freaking love this car because it's so fast and I feel free whenever we ride in it. I'm always surprised when he picks me up in it, being as though he has a wife and this car is bright yellow.

"IHOP is fine with me," I reply. I can taste those strawberry pancakes already with maple syrup. I get the same thing every time we go. Two strawberry pancakes and three orders of bacon. Yes, I love bacon, which is probably one of the many reasons why I can't get rid of this Kangaroo pouch.

We pull in the IHOP parking lot and it's not that pack for a Friday, which is a good thing. I ask the waitress to seat us in the back and wink at her. She nods her head and leads us to a booth on the far left side of the restaurant.

"What was that?" I ask Dave after we ordered and the waitress walked away.

"What?" he asked, playing dumb.

"That, back at my place with you looking at my roommate and asking her out on a date?" I ask, looking intensely in his eyes.

"Aww, my baby jealous? Don't worry baby, I only got eyes for you," he said smiling and holding my hands from across the table.

I heard someone clear their throat and when I looked up, I saw Vincent standing over me. I quickly snatched my hands away from Dave and stood up to greet Vincent. Vincent is one of my sponsors. He's about 6 feet even with silky hair because he's mixed with black and Puerto Rican. So yeah, he's two different types of crazy and has made it clear that he doesn't want me with anybody else. I'm nervous because Dave and Vincent are both glaring at each other and I'm not too sure what to do next.

Michelle

Tiffany and I went to the mall together and honestly; I only went to get my mind off of Ray. I am so tired of the way he treats me, but I love him so much. Sometimes, I think about the child we could have had together and I cry. I've cried so many tears for this man that I could cure the world of thirst. Tiffany isn't any help either, constantly bringing him up and telling me to leave him alone. She's always telling me I deserve better; like I don't already know that shit! I know I could possibly be missing out on someone better by keeping it tight for Ray. I guess I'm holding on to this tiny shred of hope that one day everything will go back to the way it was.

Well, that was yesterday and I'm going to leave the past in the past, along with my damn phone! I got so mad at Ray for not answering his phone that I threw mine into the wall like an ass! Raphael is going to be mad because I was supposed to be at work, but I drank Cîroc until I passed out last night. I'm just now able to stand up without throwing up. I would call to let him know I will be late, but I have no phone.

I drag myself out of bed to take a shower and get ready for work. Once I'm done, I hop out and lotion myself down before brushing my teeth. Thirty minutes later, I'm dressed and out the door heading to Walmart. I don't have much money and Walmart has those family mobile plans. I can spend $100 and get the phone and unlimited everything in one trip, and I can call Raphael on my way into work.

While on my way to work, I tried calling Raphael and Candy but neither of them were answering their phones. I threw my phone in the passenger seat after I realized that I have a new phone and that's probably why they weren't answering their phones.

As I was stopped at a red light, I started to have thoughts of Ray. When it's good, it's awesome but when it's bad, it's all bad. At this point, I'm not sure if the good outweighs the bad or not. Sometimes, I feel like it's time I cut my losses and move on with my life. I've given Ray too many years and tears to still be at a standstill, six years later.

I reached over and grab my phone, just as the light was turning green, so I dropped it and pulled off. The closer I get to the club, the more this strange feeling comes over me. Something doesn't feel right but I don't know what, so I pulled over onto the shoulder of the road. I'm not the smartest chick in the world but I do know that when you're having the kind of feeling I'm having right now; you do not proceed in the direction you were going.

As I'm sitting on the shoulder of the road, I hear gunshots, so I get down on the floor in my car. I'm so scared that I don't know what to do next. I hear gunshots entering my car through the windshield window as I hop in the backseat. I can feel my heart beating in my stomach, I'm so scared. I don't own a gun so I can't shoot back, and I don't even know who's shooting or why? It feels like hours have gone by when in all actuality, it was only minutes before I heard sirens and felt it was safe enough to get up. When I sat all the way up, it felt like my world was coming to an end. I hopped out of my car as fast as I could and ran all the way to the black on black Honda that I know belongs to Ray.

Before I can get close to it, it catches fire and I can hear him beating on the windows from behind the tint. I know it's never going to break because he has bulletproof windows and I drop down to the ground sobbing uncontrollably. He is dying right in front of my eyes and there's nothing I can do to help him. I'm sitting on my knees in the middle of the road watching the car burn.

"Are you okay, ma'am?" I hear someone ask me but I couldn't break my stare from the car just a few feet away from us. "Ma'am, it's going to blow, we have to move," the paramedic said. I could hear her but I couldn't move. I started to feel woozy. I could feel my body swaying before everything went dark.

Beep... Beep... Beep... Beep... Beep... Beep... Beep... Beep... Beep... Beep... Beep

I woke up to a beeping noise. Judging by the noise and the brightness, I could tell I was in the hospital. I slowly opened my eyes and got an instant headache. When I reached my hand up to stroke my head, I noticed it was wrapped. I tried to sit up but the pain in my stomach stopped me dead in my tracks. I flipped the cover back and my stomach was also wrapped. I'm confused.

"Good morning. I'm Jennifer, your nurse for today. Are feeling any discomfort?" asked my nurse as I nodded my head.

"My... head... my... stomach," I struggled to get out. My throat was so dry I couldn't even swallow. "Water," I croaked out. My nurse gave me my hospital jug of water and it felt like heaven going down!

"Why am I here? What happened? How long have I been here?" I rambled out once I was able to talk.

"We'll start with the easiest question. Today is Tuesday, so you've been here for four days. You are here because you were shot in the stomach. The bullet went straight through. You passed out and hit your head on the ground," she explained and all the memories hit me at once. I started crying real hard, making my head hurt even worse.

I could clearly remember pulling over because of the bad feelings I was having. I remember seeing Ray's car flip over and explode before he even had a chance to attempt to get out.

"Shhh sweetie, you're fine. Everything is going to be ok," she said, rubbing the top of my head. "Ray, where is he? Is he ok?" I ask.

"I don't know Ray sweetie, you were in the car alone," she replied.

"No, you don't understand. I need to see Ray. I need to make sure he's ok! Please, help me find him," I begged but she just looked at me with sad eyes.

My monitors started beeping like crazy and Nurse Jennifer was trying to calm me down. "Sweetie, you have to relax," was the last thing I heard before I passed out.

"How is she?" I heard someone ask.

"She's fine. She's just overwhelmed with emotions right now. She kept asking about someone named Ray. Maybe you can find him for her and she will be ok." I heard Nurse Jennifer say.

"Naw, she need to leave him wherever he's at! I'm tired of my cousin crying because of him," the voice I now recognize as Tiffany says.

"Excuse me. Sorry for interrupting. Mrs. Jennifer, I'm Tamia and I'm supposed to shadow you today for clinicals." I heard a different voice say. I opened my eyes slightly and I can't believe how pretty she is. I can tell she has a cute shape, even in her scrubs. She looks about my age, so she can't be a nurse already.

"Who are you?" I ask, startling everyone in the room. I watch as Tamia walks over to me.

"My name is Tamia and I will be shadowing your nurse, Mrs. Jennifer today," she says with a smile. I nod my head. "Ok, I'm going to check your vitals now, ok Michelle?" she says. It's more like she's asking if it's ok with me, so I nod my head. I watch her as she checks my blood pressure and temperature. She turned towards nurse Jennifer and said, "18". When she turned back to me I was looking confused. "The amount of breaths you took in that minute," she explained.

"Oh. I didn't know you were counting," I said.

"Yes ma'am, that's because I never tell anyone when I'm counting their breaths. Had I told you, you would have subconsciously changed it up, whether faster or slower," she said.

"Oh ok, cool," I said.

"It was nice meeting you. I have other vitals to catch up on, but I will come back in a few hours, if that's ok with you," she said.

"Yes, that's fine," I said and she turned to walk out of the door.

I looked at Tiffany and she was frowning looking at the door but quickly wiped it away when she noticed I was looking at her. "She's a natural," I said to Nurse Jennifer, who smiled in return. "So, she looks my age, is she a nurse already?" I asked my nurse.

"Mind your own damn business, Chelle!" said Tiffany, snapping on me.

"Well, I was just curious," I replied.

"Not curious enough to ask her your damn self," said Tiffany. She had a point but I didn't want to offend someone who was assigned to take care of me. Hell, she might decide not to give me any of my medicine!

"Actually no, she's not a nurse just yet. She graduates in a few months in Health Administration and one of the requirements is to shadow an RN for 200 hours. She's starting early, so she will not be pressed when it's time. Don't worry, you're in good hands. She has taken all of the classes necessary to take the nursing board exam if she wanted to," Nurse Jennifer answered my question.

Tiffany listened until Mrs. Jennifer finished talking before storming out of the room. "I don't know what her problem is," I stated and Mrs. Jennifer just shook her head before leaving as well.

Rashard

I grabbed my Boost mobile phone that, I along with my team captains, had and chirped each of them telling them to surround each truck and disarm them without making noise. It took about thirty minutes for them to complete their first mission and I must say that I was impressed.

"Raphael, I want you to approach Brittany's brother and say, 'we have your sister, tell your men to stand down'," I said to Raphael on the phone.

"What?! Man, they ain't finna punk me! I say you let me blast these fools, Shard!" Raphael responded angrily.

"It's not about being punked. It's about being smart. My men are outside with their men but in here, it's one against four and a whole bunch of people that has nothing to do with this," I said calmly into the phone receiver.

"Alright man," Raphael said defeated.

I turned to look at the monitors, so I could watch the interaction. Raphael walked right up to him and said exactly what I told him to say. We never disconnected the call, so I could hear everything I needed to hear. I watched closely as the gunman clenched his jaw muscles and balled his hands into a fist. Raphael took a step back and turned around attempting to walk away. "Never turn your back on someone angry," I said to Raphael.

Before he had a chance to turn back towards him, the gunman hit him in the back of the head. "Fuck!" I said out loud to myself.

"You want me to help him, boss?" Candy asked and for a second, I forgot she was even here.

"Look under Raphael's chair. There is a rifle there with a scope," I paused to glance back at the monitors and saw that Raphael and the gunman were going at it! Blow for blow! I looked at another monitor and saw the gunman that was watching the VIP Booths leave his post, heading towards the fight but the one that was supposed to be watching Candy left his to stop him.

"I got it boss. What's next?" Candy asked. Thinking fast, I knew this was Candy's only shot simply because no one was watching her or whomever their target is in the VIP Booth.

"Open the third drawer and close it completely three times, and hit the button that will appear," I told her.

"Damn boss, you got shit everywhere," she said as I heard the slot opening, giving her a clear view of her mark.

"Stick your rifle out and kill the two guys in all black that are fussing. One of them was supposed to be watching you and the other watching the VIP Booths," I said.

A few seconds after I turned back towards the monitor, Candy swiftly took down both gunman. "Two down, two to go," I spoke into the receiver.

"Not for long," Raphael said.

"Raph man, you can't kill him right now. Too many witnesses," I responded to Raph.

"Self-defense," he said out of breath. I could tell he was getting winded. I knew just how to help him without being seen.

"Candy, leave," I spoke into the receiver.

"Boss, I never question you but I can't," she replied.

"Candy. Leave," I said through clenched teeth. I watched her walk out of Raphael's office heading towards the front door. "No, go through the side underground exit. The code is 2243. There's a dark green Honda parked with the keys in the ignition. Get in and drive south out of the club parking lot. Once you're stopped by the wall, the code is 1143 and the wall will move. You will have 15 seconds to go through before the wall closes back up. Go home and I'll call you later," I said to Candy as I watch her do as she's told. All the training I took her through did numbers on her once extremely hard headed ass!

"Raph, do you have your vest on?" I asked Raphael once Candy was in the car.

"Always," he responded right before being slammed on the table.

"On the count of three, roll to your right, pass three tables and crawl under the fourth one as fast as you can. Bullets are about to fly. When you're under the table, push the green button and hold your breath. 1... 2... 3," I explained.

Slowly, I typed a series of codes into my computer, releasing sub machine guns from the ceiling. I don't want to shoot any of my guests, so I keep them trained on the wall. I hit the yellow button, so only pellets will come out of them. I looked for Raphael on the monitors and saw the table slowly coming back up after taking Raphael underground.

"Raph, you good?" I asked because he should have asked for a code by now. I pause, waiting on him to respond but he didn't. His ass didn't hold his breath. *Fuck!* I think to myself as I hit the blue button under my desk, sending oxygen throughout the underground area to wake him all the way up. I told him to hold his breath because I knew when he hit the button to go underground, it was going to trap him and suck all of the oxygen out of it. It also releases some type of chemical that can knock a bull out. All he had to do was listen to me.

I glanced at the monitors and saw everyone that was chilling thirty minutes ago, running around frantically trying to escape without getting hit by a pellet. I searched each monitor looking for the remaining two gunmen, and one was out and the other ran out of the side door.

I buzzed the VIP Booths' intercom systems to pick up their frequency. "Bruh, you think all that is for you?" I heard a voice say.

"Shit, probably so. Fuck! I hope whoever taking mufuckers down take all them bitches down," another voice responded.

"What if they kill all of the people stopping them and come in?" the first voice asked, sounding scared as fuck.

"Well shit, they ain't gone be able to get in here. You see all that shit ole girl had to do to bring us up here," the other voice responded.

I zoomed in on their booth but their backs were turned away from the camera. I'll tell you one thing though, if they thought they were about to be saved on my damn time without putting in work, they had another thing coming. I sent the regular elevator through the elevator chambers to release the VIP guests without them seeing me. I watched them look around at each other after the elevators' doors opened and nobody moved to get on.

"These booths are going to blow up in five minutes." I lied into the intercom system and everyone rushed to get on the elevators. I sent the elevators down to the dance floor, so everyone could get off and leave.

I cursed myself for not checking with my team as I switched the surveillance to the outside cameras. All hell had broken loose. Bodies were everywhere! I scanned the monitors for Dre and found him off to the side, chopping bodies up. This nigga is beyond sick!

"Man, what the fuck you do to me?" I heard someone ask. It took me a minute to figure out it was Raphael waking up.

"You didn't hold your breath," I replied simply.

"Shit, all the rolling took my breath man. You can't hold shit you out of yo!" he screamed in my ear.

"Then you should have caught it before you hit the damn button!" I snapped on him. "Say 1734," I said to Raphael.

"Man, you got contraptions and tunnels everywhere, bruh!" Raphael replied after being released from his holding spot.

"It's important to stay ready. That way, you never have to get ready. There's a purple Honda right outside the door as soon as you crank it up repeat 1734. The parking spot will lower, taking you into a tunnel. Drive through and when you come out you will be on the opposite side of town. Go home," I said to Raphael, disconnecting the call.

Now that I got my people out safe, I need to get myself out. I head back the way I came in to hop back in my all black Honda. I know you're thinking this nigga got Honda's all over the place and yes, you're right. It's because the police will pull over a bubble Caprice, box Chevy, or something flashy long before they will pull over a Honda Accord. It's the safest getaway car.

Anyway, I drive back above ground to exit out the front entrance. As I'm driving, I see Dre fall to the ground and a gunman is heading in his direction. Without thinking about consequences, I hop out of my car and run full speed towards the gunman. It wasn't until I got near him that I realized I didn't grab my gun, so I tackled him. Once we were both on the ground, I sat on his chest and tried to beat his face in.

All of a sudden I'm being lifted off the gunman and when I look back, it's Dre. He shoots the guy in the face and we both turn to see the fourth gunman from inside the club, hopping in my car and pulling off. Dre instantly started shooting. At first, he was missing because the nigga had blood dripping in his eyes! Not wanting him to let dude get away, I snatched my shirt off and wiped his face. The very next bullet hit the back of the car and then he shot the back tire and homeboy lost control. I sat there watching my car flip and a few minutes later, it blew up, pissing me all the way off.

"Man, why the fuck you blow up my car?!" I screamed at Dre.

"Nigga, it's a Honda, go buy another one, hell. At least dude don't get to steal it," he said laughing as we walked away. I hopped in the truck with him and we drove out the back entrance heading towards my downtown three-bedroom condo.

"This bitch nice!" Dre said and for a moment, I forgot he didn't know I'm the boss. Shit, he should see my house! I'm here most of the time though. Each room has a walk in closet and full bathroom. The guest bathroom is in the hallway. The kitchen is huge! All I need is a bad bitch that can cook and we will be great! This place has a living room, dining room and den as well. I only smoke in the sunroom because I don't want my shit smelling like weed. The walls are cream but every piece of furniture I have is black.

I head to my room to take a shower and change after I showed Dre where he could go and do the same because it wouldn't be long before we decided to head out. I needed to know who was in that VIP Booth and who wanted to kill him.

The next day, I still couldn't reach Chelle so she could do my damn dreads over but Tiffany's ratchet ass been blowing my phone up, pissing me off. I haven't even answered for her because I know she don't want shit. If it was that important she would leave a voicemail or send a text message like normal people, but nooo. This bitch wants to call back to back, then take a break just to start calling again.

I called my mom to see if she would do my hair and she said yes, so I headed to her house to jump fresh. My brother, Bo was there and I had to give him a quick rundown of what went down at the club, without telling him exactly how everybody escaped. I already don't trust many people. Hell, I can name all of the people I trust and let's just say, Bo didn't make that list. He has too many shady tendencies in these streets and I know it doesn't stop there. The only reason he has never crossed me is because I've never given him a reason to.

It took my mom all of thirty minutes to retwist my dreads. I'm thinking about coming to her from now on because it takes Chelle's ass a couple of hours each week! That's time I can be chasing money instead of being cooped up in her place all that time.

"Say ma, how about I come over once a week and you retwist my hair for me?" I ask.

"No sir! I'm not trying to spend my Saturdays doing hair anymore. I spoiled you when I started them for you and when you moved out, that cleared me of those duties. Where is the girl that's been doing it?" my mom replied.

"I don't know ma. Plus, I don't want her to do it anymore," I reply back.

"Why not?" she asks with her hands on her hip.

"Because it takes her hours to do it and it just took you thirty minutes," I answered, and she laughed while walking away, shaking her head.

I followed behind her into the kitchen. I watched as she seasoned the meat so it can marinate over night for Sunday dinner. "What's funny?" I ask.

"Hmmm, you don't get it, do you son?" she answered, confusing the fuck out of me. I just shook my head no because I have no idea.

"Son, are you dating her?" she asked.

"No ma'am," I replied.

"Have you ever dated her in the past? Or have you slept with her before?" she asked. I took a second before I answered because these are trick questions coming from her. If I answer honestly, she might hit me but if I lie, she's going to hit me.

"It's Michelle that's been doing my hair," I say, taking a seat on the stool. I was looking down when she walked up to me, slapping in the back in my head.

See, back in the day I was seeing her heavy until she acted like she was pregnant by me. I knew good and damn well she wasn't because I've always taken the necessary precautions, so I wouldn't be a father before I was ready. This bitch decided to embarrass herself, trying to surprise me with some shit I knew was a lie. If she was actually pregnant, it was a 100% chance it wasn't mine. Now, if she believed it was mine she would have kept it, but she knew like I knew, it wasn't mine. See, a bitch will try to get over on you if you let her. I'm not that nigga though.

After that, I realized I couldn't trust her either because she was sleeping with more than me to get pregnant in the first place, so I all but cut her off. There were no more dates, quality time, talking on the phone or whatever. I still smash her from time to time but that's because of how she dresses when I come to get my hair did. Not to mention, it's always her trying to fuck me. I just give her what she wants. If I can get my mom to do my hair, I'd cut her off completely.

"Why are you still dealing with her Rashard?" my mom asked me, clearly pissed off.

"Because she does my hair," I answered because to me, it was just that simple.

"Baby, you can't play with people's feelings like that. I'd hate to go to jail for killing her because she killed you. If I'm in jail, who's going to cook Sunday dinner?" she asked seriously, causing me to crack up with laughter.

She didn't even crack a smile and that shut me right on up. "Ma, I'm not playing with her feelings. I don't even talk to her like that anymore," I say to my mom.

"Are you still sleeping with her?" she asked. "Exactly! You're playing with her feelings!" she yelled before I could answer the question. "Baby, women don't have sex without emotions. Well, most women won't and that girl loves you. She's doing whatever she can to keep you around, even if it's for a little while. It shouldn't take anyone more than an hour to retwist dreads. It's taking her so long because she's using that time to spend with you," she said before walking out of the kitchen.

I didn't follow her this time because I was sitting on the bar stool looking stupid thinking about what she said. I never thought it was taking Chelle that long because she didn't want me to leave. I gotta cut this bitch off right now and I'll just find a hair shop to go to. Naw, fuck a shop, I'll find another bitch on campus that do hair as a hustle.

I decided to crash at my mom's place so I'd be here for Sunday dinner. Plus, I knew she would get up cooking and I couldn't chance being distracted and not being able to make it. Bo stayed in his old room too. My mom has a five-bedroom house and we all had our own rooms. She left everything the way we left it and since we all occasionally stay over; we have clothes here. We are all two years apart with me being the youngest at twenty-three. Myra is twenty-five, Ashley is twenty-seven and Bo is twenty-nine. I pretty much help out the most because Bo ain't doing much with himself.

Ashley is dark skinned like myself and she works at Sears. She has two daughters, Iyanna who is three and Jamila, who just turned five. Myra has a caramel complexion and she works as a CNA at a local nursing home. Bo work's at our uncle Leroy's car shop and has a daughter named Diane, who is five and a son name Robert, who is also five. They aren't twins, he has two baby mamas. I've met the kids and they look just like him but he has never brought their moms around the family at all.

Myra and Ashley pulled up at the same time around lunch time with their kids. I haven't seen them since last week and I missed them. My nieces and nephew, not my sisters. I walk out the door and as soon as Michael sees me, he snatches away from Myra, running at me full speed. Once he's in arm's length, I scoop him up, giving him a nuggie as he tries to squirm away.

Ashley keeps Iyana and Jamila strapped down so tight that it takes her a minute to get them out of the car. Jamila makes it to me first and I grab her, spinning her around in circles before putting her down. She fell about four times before she gave up and sat on the ground swaying. Iyana finally made it to me and I couldn't resist kissing and biting on her chubby cheeks. Iyana is my baby girl! I love all of them the same but I think Iyana likes me more than them. She follows me around every time we're here and she won't take a nap unless I'm holding her. It's been that way since she was born.

We all walk back inside, so the kids can speak to their granny. I have no idea why my mom wants them calling her granny when she's only forty-nine. I walk in to my mom sitting in the kitchen looking at an old picture of her, my aunt Jennifer, and uncle Leroy. My mom, Monique, worked all of our lives so as soon as I got on, I started paying bills and depositing money into her bank account. I always paid the bank manager to tell her it was a gift from the bank for being such a loyal client. She would never spend the money though. She thought it was too good to be, so she activated a new account just for her gifts. She was working as a custodian and only bringing home about $700 every other week. Once the gifts got to 2 million dollars without her checking the balance, she quit her job. Her gifts are steady growing.

"Hey Granny!" Iyanna, Jamila and Michael say, running past me into the kitchen.

"Hey, Granny babies!" she yelled, hopping down to hug and kiss on them. "How are you guys liking school?" she asked them, climbing her short ass back on the stool.

"I love it Granny!" Jamila said. Michael just nodded his in agreement and Iyanna made her way back to me.

"You don't want to talk to Granny?" my mom asked Iyanna.

"I want Unc," she replied softly, pulling at my shirt for me to pick her up. I looked at my mom and she was smiling. These Sunday dinners keep her sane.

"Ma, where's Bo?" I asked because I hadn't seen him all morning and I know we both stayed here last night.

"He's up in his room. You know how he is. He will be down when the food is ready," she replied. I just shook my head. Bo seriously need counseling the way he needs attention. It has to be someone that can help him get over that need.

"I have a surprise for you guys. Follow me," I said to the kids. My mom didn't know about it either, so she yelled for Ashley and Myra to come to the backyard too.

"Close your eyes." I turned to them all to say as we rounded the corner to the backyard.

"SURPRISE!" I yelled as I stood back smiling. The kids started jumping up and down before running off to go play.

"Boy, who sold you a spacewalk?" Ashley asked yelling.

"Yeah who and can you buy one for my yard too?" Myra joined in causing us all to laugh.

"Some Mexicans were moving from a location and selling everything out of the old one. For some reason, they had this spacewalk and when I climbed in, I noticed it had a rock climbing side. I climbed up and that's when I realized it was a slide on the other side. They only wanted $75 for it, so I bought it and put it in the shed," I explained. When I looked at mom, her eyes were watery. "Don't you start woman!" I said to her as we all laughed.

We played until it was dinner time. After we ate, surprisingly without any arguments, everyone left and went home. I had to stay behind to put the spacewalk up for the night. By the time I got home, I was dead to the world.

When I woke up the next morning, I had messages from everybody. I got out of bed, brushed my teeth, and hopped in the shower. I threw on a t-shirt and some sweatpants because I have class from 9 until 11 then from 1 until 2 and football practice at 3. I'll be on campus all day today and I'm not too thrilled about it.

Tiffany: So you ignoring me?

Tiffany: Hello?????

Tiffany: Rashard!

Tiffany: Well fuck you then I won't hit you up no more.

Chardae: We need to meet up and talk about this Shard. I didn't make this baby by myself.

Candy: Just making sure you're good boss man

Dre: aye bruh everybody straight

Tiffany: I'm sorry plz call me back

I read my messages shaking my head at Tiffany and Chardae. Tiffany seriously bugging and Chardae got to know I ain't dumb enough to get her nothing ass pregnant. I'm really careful out here in these streets.

Rashard: I'm good Candy.

Rashard: Iight bet Bruh. Practice @ 3

I ignored Tiffany and Chardae because them hoes ain't talking about nothing. I know Chardae wants a relationship but she need to work on getting herself together first. Like I said before, I don't have time to fix her when I'm not right myself. As far as Tiffany goes, that crazy bitch is cut off. She's not the only bitch with a good head on her shoulders.

Tamia

After that awkward exchange between Armani, her sponsor, and myself, I went in my room to jump start my day. By the time I finished getting dressed, Armani and her dude were gone. I checked my phone and I had a voicemail. Calling my voice message, I began to listen to my messages.

"Good morning, this is Nicole Jackson calling for Tamia Anderson. This is in reference to both your paper exam and skills test. I normally do not discuss grades over the phone but since you did so well, I didn't think you would mind. Your score for your paper exam is 110 because you got the bonus question correct. You scored a 97 on your nursing skills test. This give you an overall average test score of 103.5! You should be proud of yourself. Do not return to class. For the remainder of the year, you will shadow different nurses at The Detroit Medical Center. After your total 200 hours are complete, you will meet the state board qualifications to become a registered nurse as well health administrator. Nurse Jennifer is expecting you today at 3. Good luck!"

By the end of the voicemail, I was in tears. I did it! I can't believe I actually did it! One thing for certain and two things for sure; I wouldn't be here without God, and I give all thanks and glory to the big man upstairs! I could have given up a long time ago but he didn't let me. I could have fallen victim to the streets like so many girls my age, but he wouldn't let me. I could be dead but he saw a purpose for me to still be here, and I promise I won't stop! "Thank you Jesus for all you have done and for everything you are about to do," I say out loud.

I thought I had class at 9 but since I don't have any more classes at all, I'm so glad! I now get to try some hands on stuff at the hospital. I really hope Nurse Jennifer is nice, simply because it will make my job that much easier.

I head down to campus anyway because I don't have anything to do around the house. I would normally be content with the couch and Netflix, but I'm far too excited to sit still.

Once I get to campus, I head straight for the field house. I'm walking and singing, looking up at the sky.

Never would have made it
Never could have made it without you
I would have lost it all
But now I see how you were there for me
And I can say
Never would have made it
Never could have made it without you
I would have lost it all
But now I see
How you were there for me
And I can say
I'm stronger, I'm wiser
I'm better, much better
When I look back
over all you brought me through
I can see that you were the one I held on to
And I never, never would have made it
Oh, I never could have made
Oh, I would have lost it all
Oh, but now I see
How you were there for me

I never would have made it
No, never
Never could have made it without you
I would've lost my mind
A long time ago!
If it had not been you
I am stronger
I am wiser
And now I am better
So much better
I made it
Through my storm and my test
Because you were there
To carry me through my mess
I am stronger
I am wiser
I can stand here and tell you
I made it
Anybody out there that can say that you made it?
I'm stronger
I'm wiser
I'm better
Much better
I made it
I made it
never would have made it
never could have made it
I would have lost my mind
I would have gave up
But you were right there
you were right there
I never would have made it
Oh I never could have made it without you
Somebody just need to testify this tonight
Next to them tell them
I am stronger, I am wiser

I am better, much better
When I look back
Over what he brought me through
I realize that I made it
Because I had you to hold on to
Now I am stronger, now I am wiser
I am better, so much better
I've made it
Is there anybody in this house other than me
That could declare you made it
Tell your neighbor
never would have made it
Tell 'em never could have made it
Oh, I wish I had some help here
I wish I had just two or three people
That would just declare it
Never would have made it
never could have made it without you
I just, I just love to encourage myself
Sometime I look in the mirror and say
I'm stronger, I'm wiser
I am better, so much better
When I look back over what he brought me
through
I realize that I made it
because I had you to hold on to
But I never would have made it
I never could have made it without you
When I look back over
What He brought me through
I realize that I made it
Because I had You to hold on to

I didn't realize I had stopped walking. I was standing in the middle of campus with my eyes closed singing and crying. Marvin Sapp know he touched me with that song! When I opened them up, there was a crowd of people surrounding me clapping. I was so embarrassed. I could only imagine how stupid I looked, standing in one spot singing and crying loud enough for people to gather around. They are probably only clapping because I stopped singing.

I was stuck probably looking dumber with my mouth wide open. I could feel my tears falling freely.

"Excuse me, Miss Lady." I heard someone say from behind me. When I turned around, it was Rashard. My breath got caught in my throat and my panties got wet.

"Yes?" I answered.

"You sound beautiful," he said, handing me some tissue. I grabbed them and wiped my face.

"Thanks Rashard," I replied while walking away.

I wanted to run like hell away from this man that gave me butterflies. It's been years since I felt this way. Well I take that back, I've never felt like this without actually knowing a person first. The scary part about dating now is I actually have time now that I don't have any more classes. The more time I invest in a person, the more feelings I'm able to invest.

I think it was so easy leaving Amere the way I did because I never truly invested my all into him because I was putting my all in the books. So, when he went out and made a baby with another woman, it was the best thing that could have happened to me. I would have been going to Community College on the coast and stuck cooking meals for a man who didn't appreciate me had he not done that. Not saying anything is bad about Community College because it isn't. All I'm saying is sometimes you have to get away from certain people to grow. Especially, when you're on different paths.

I glanced back and the crowd had dispersed but Rashard was still standing there watching me. I smiled and waved him over. He started jogging in my direction. I got so nervous all of a sudden and my hands started to clam up.

"How are you doing, Miss Lady?" he asked, once he caught up with me.

"I'm great actually," I responded with a smile.

"That's what's up. What was that about, if you don't mind me asking?" he asked.

"I've had an extremely tough life. Nobody knows what I really went through growing up because I haven't told anyone, not even my best friend. I've worked so hard to get this far and I only have three more months left before I graduate. I got a call this morning from the health advisory directory telling me I didn't have to return to class because I scored so high on my exams. I'll be doing clinicals until graduation!" I told him excitedly.

I was smiling so big and trying to contain myself from jumping up and down. Then I noticed he hadn't responded. He was just staring at me and I couldn't read that expression. My smile slowly faded. I realized I just boasted to someone that could be going through it. I didn't mean to brag but I'm extremely proud of what I've accomplished.

"I'm sorry," I said taking a step away from him. I was about to haul ass I was so embarrassed and I think he knew it. He grabbed my hand and turned me back around.

"For what?" he asked, looking in my eyes. His gaze was so intense, I looked away. He grabbed my chin and turned my head, forcing me to look back up at him. I felt a tingling feeling go through my whole body before I shied away from his gaze again.

"Look at me, Tamia," he said sternly. The way my name rolled off of his tongue did something to me. I slowly looked him in his eyes. "What are you sorry for?" he asked again.

"For blabbering on about my accomplishments," I responded.

"No, you were telling me how you beat all odds and you're still doing it. I wouldn't have asked you if I didn't want to know," he said shutting my little ass right on up. I love for a nigga to take control and that's exactly what he was doing. I don't even know why I became so shy all of a sudden when you normally can't pay me not to speak my mind.

"Why haven't you used my number?" he asked, frowning just a little bit. It caught me completely off guard because I forgot I had his number. I've thought about him from time to time this week but shit, it's only been a few days since he gave me his number.
"I don't know. I haven't really thought-"

"You haven't thought about me?" he cut me off, clearly offended.

"Yes."

"Well, why did you lie?" he asked still frowning.

"Listen Rashard, I didn't lie! If you would have allowed me to finish what I was saying, you would have heard the rest of it. I haven't use your number because I haven't thought about it. It being your number! Did you forget that right after you gave it to me, I got my ass handed to me?" I asked now pissed.

I looked up at him watching his frown turn into a smirk. "Well, give me yours," he demanded, handing me his phone. Without thinking about it, I entered my number and saved it as T. "Who the fuck is T, Miss Lady?" he asked smiling. I didn't respond. I just looked at him trying to find the humor in it. "You're not a fucking nigga. Your name is Tamia, not T," he said playing with his phone.

"What are you doing?" I asked.

"Changing your name to your name," he replied, matter of factly.

"C'mon and walk me to the field house, so I can do a few laps," I said shocking myself.

We walked to the track together getting to know each other. It wasn't much to tell about myself since I had already told him everything briefly. I did tell him about Armani. Well, not about her sponsors or anything like that, but I mentioned we lived together. He didn't seem too pleased with the fact that I have a roommate.

I learned he is the youngest of four. His mother raised them alone, and he has two nieces and a nephew. I already knew he played football.

He ran alongside me as I ran around the track giving me pointers since he saw my last race. I almost told him he's the reason I lost. Well, his dick print is. I was in the lead and had I not slowed down when I did, Alexus wouldn't have caught me. I didn't though. I just kept that tidbit of information to myself. I wasn't going to be running track much longer anyway. First thing Monday morning, I was going to the administration building to see if I could stop without losing my scholarship so close to the end of the year.

Rashard and I sat on the bleachers talking until 2. He told me I caused him to miss two of his classes, but he's the one that should be more focused because I would not have missed a class for conversation. It doesn't matter how good it is. He's lucky I don't live far from campus or the hospital, since I have to be there at 3.

He walked me to my car and wished me luck on my first day of work. After I got in my car, he still hadn't walked away so I rolled the window down. I smiled because he didn't say anything. "I gotta go," I said to him. He smiled and leaned in the car kissing my forehead. It felt so good to allow someone to give me attention. I hope he's ready because I am and I only want him!

I got home in record speed but Armani still wasn't there. I could tell she hadn't been there at all because it was still clean. I hopped in the shower and headed to the hospital. After I got there, I had to go get a badge made, then swipe it on the volunteer time clock. I approached the nurses and introduced myself. Everyone was pretty nice and welcoming. I told them I was there to shadow a nurse named Jennifer. A CNA tech name Lola told she was in room 2101, and that I should go on in and start shadowing.

What they didn't know is I've been a CNA since I was 12. My mom got really sick and couldn't take care of herself, let alone me! That's why I was emancipated so early. I had to prove to my mom that I was responsible enough to take care of us both. After six months of her not getting any better, I told her if she passed before the paperwork was complete that I'd be stuck in the system until I was 18. After I told her that, we had the paperwork drawn up, went before a judge and right after my 13th birthday, I was legally an adult. Not long after that, she passed away. All I had to do so the state wouldn't reverse it was maintain our apartment. I kept it clean and stocked with everything I needed. I still went to school and every time my case worker came to see me, she would cry. I didn't know why then but I know now that she was proud of me.

Lola wanted to give me a walk-through of the hospital but they had signs everywhere, so I didn't need her to walk me around pointing. She seemed a bit offended but I'm here to work, not make friends.

I walked in the room with confidence in every stride. I introduced myself to Mrs. Jennifer and the patient, completely ignoring the other woman because she was staring at me like I slapped her mama or some shit. After checking the patient's vitals, I excused myself to go and check vitals on the other patients to save Mrs. Jennifer some work, since Lola was sitting on her ass. I was on a roll zooming in and out of the rooms and charting everything into the system. When I came out of the second room, I saw ole girl from my first patient's room storming out.

She looked so dumb storming off in the wrong direction. She got to the end of the hall, which was a dead end and damn near slipped turning around with all of that attitude. "How the fuck do I get outta here?" she asked storming past me. I took a second to weigh my options before I responded because I wanted to pop this bitch, but I needed these hours to graduate. "Do you know or are you dumb?" she said, interrupting my thoughts.

"Can you read?" I asked pointing at the sign right above where we were standing, which was pointing in the direction of the elevators. She looked up and stormed off again.

When I turned around, Mrs. Jennifer was standing at the door watching the interaction. "I'm sorry Mrs. Jennifer-,"

"Don't worry about it baby. I don't think she liked you from the moment you walked in her cousin's room," Mrs. Jennifer said interrupting me. I smiled because I couldn't tell her what I was thinking, which is had we been anywhere else, she'd be on the floor!

The rest of the day was a pretty good day. I was beyond tired when I got home. The apartment was still clean so that meant Armani still hadn't been home. I walked to her room to be sure and she had dirty clothes everywhere, but I didn't see what she wore this morning. I called her three times but she didn't answer. Her ass probably staying with one of her sponsors tonight.

Tamia: Hey Mani. Haven't seen or talked to you all day. Call or text me when you get this

We don't call or text each other because we live together and we come home every night. I'm a little worried because she usually drops in a few times throughout the day. Normally, I'll go to class and come home for lunch, and there is something to clean, whether it be dishes or clothes from one of her many rendezvous. I walk back into the kitchen so I can cook dinner and put me a plate in the refrigerator for lunch tomorrow.

Rashard: How are you, miss lady?

I glanced at my phone seeing the text message from Rashard and my heart skipped a beat! I started pacing because I didn't know what to say. After thinking about how dumb I looked walking back and forth, I decided to respond. My problem is I haven't dated anyone seriously since Amere. Then, I don't know what Rashard wants out of this.

Tamia: I'm fine. How are you Sir?

I started prepping the meat for my meatloaf. The kitchen is my safe haven. It's the only place I am 100% comfortable.

Rashard: I'm good Miss Lady. Wyd? Want some company?

Tamia: I'm cooking dinner. What kind of phone do you have?

Rashard: IPhone

Tamia: I'm going to turn my location on so you can find me.

Rashard: iight

I forgot to turn my music on while I cook and sanitize the house. As soon as I pressed play, *7/11* by Beyoncé started playing. I absolutely love this song! It makes me so happy and energetic but I have no idea why because she isn't really saying much. So, I decide to make everything really simple. Meatloaf, mashed potatoes and gravy, and sweet peas. After the meatloaf was finished, I started *7/11* over so I could clean the kitchen. I walked around cleaning up and dancing until there was a knock on my door.

I walked towards the door peeking through the peephole but whoever it was, was standing off to the side. "Who is it?" I yelled.

"Rashard." I heard him respond to me. I opened the door, stepping to the side so he could enter. He walked in looking around and nodding his head.

"Shall I give you a tour?" I asked and watched as he nodded his head.

I walked him through our two-bedroom apartment without opening Armani's room door, since her room is never company ready. "Y'all keep it nice and clean in here," he said to me. I so badly wanted to correct him but I decided against it.

"I'm about to fix me a plate, would you like something to eat?" I asked standing to my feet. He nodded his head without asking me what I cooked. I sure as hell hope he isn't allergic to anything. We ate in the living room while watching *Revenge* on Netflix until we both fell asleep.

Armani

So, I'm sitting here nervously looking back and forth between Dave and Vincent. I stood up quickly clearing my throat while trying to think of what to say. I was stuck on stupid. Literally! I continued to glance back and forth hoping somebody would say something but they continued to stare each other down.

"Vincent. How have you been? When did you get back in town?" I asked Vincent trying to break the ice.

"This morning. I was coming to surprise you after I left here so imagine my surprise," he said, never breaking his stare down with Dave. It's like they were having a who's the man contest and whoever looked away first wasn't one. I could only shake my head because I didn't know what else to say. Honestly, I didn't want to be involved with Vincent anymore, but I didn't know how to tell him.

Vincent is a very crazy and dangerous man with a quick temper. I've seen him kill niggas for less and I think he has invested some type of feelings in me. His crazy ass has told me on more than one occasion that he doesn't want me dealing with anyone else. I always agree because the nigga got good dick! Hell, I'll say anything you want me to say when you fucking me right.

"Who is this?" Dave asked like his ass ain't married.

"Vincent. His name is Vincent. Vincent, this is Dave," I said introducing them. These niggas didn't even acknowledge anything I said because they were still staring each other down. I'm like come on now, I have shit to do today! We were supposed to eat breakfast so he could take me back home.

"Let's go," Vincent said holding his hand out to me. I looked at him but he was still staring at Dave. I then looked at his hand like he has the plague. These niggas need to learn that I don't belong to no fucking body. I can date and fuck whoever I want because I'm single! I don't love these niggas; I fuck these niggas and spend their money. All of my situationships are simple to me. I give you pussy and time, and they pay my half on everything and keep my bank account looking good.

"Naw, Vincent. I'm about to eat my breakfast and go home. I'll hit you up later," I said feeling myself. Never in the twenty-three years that I've been on this planet have I had men fighting over me. They really don't even know me, so I guess they are fighting over this good pussy. I know Vincent is crazy but I'm here with Dave and he's not going to let anything happen to me.

"Let's go. Now!" he said through clenched teeth. I almost stood up but the glare Dave gave me planted my ass right back in my seat. I swear I don't know how the fuck I keep attracting these crazy ass men!

"She's about to have breakfast. After that, I'm taking her home. She will call you later," Dave said to Vincent. Dave made a grave mistake. I understand he's a man and Vincent is disrespecting him in a major way, but you have to know how to read people. First of all, Vincent ain't the type of dude you check while he's mad. Second of all, if you gone check a man like Vincent while he's mad, then you need to stand up because he will hit you.

"The only reason I'm not going to shoot you right here is because we're in a public place, and I don't have enough bullets to lay everybody in here down. So, let this be your warning boy, don't speak unless spoken to," Vincent said to Dave.

"Man, check this-," Dave started but was cut off by a fist to his jaw. I hopped out of my chair and stepped away from the fight. These niggas were tearing this damn restaurant up, throwing each other into tables and some more shit. I was pissed beyond measurement.

I walked around the fight heading towards the door. I quickly flagged down a cab, so I could go home. It was fairly easy because the cab was parked idly, waiting on a cab fare. The cabbie was driving extremely slow and I was getting text message after text message! I didn't read any of them because I knew Vincent was cursing my ass out. I needed to get to my house, get some clothes, and go stay at a hotel a few days, so he could cool off without knowing where I was. I knew he would be mad and probably jump on Tamia's ass but hell, she ain't ever lost a fight before, so I'm almost sure she could hold her own.

"Can I get you to speed up? I'm kind of pressed for time," I asked the cabbie. He completely ignored me. He didn't even look through the rearview mirror at me. It was as if I hadn't said a thing to him. "Sir?" I called out and waited. A few seconds passed and he still hadn't said anything to me. His phone began to ring and I waited to see if he would answer and he did.

"Hello... yes sir... right outside of Waffle House... alright, be there shortly," he said hanging up.

"Who was that?" I asked. "Were you talking about me? Where are you taking me?" I asked question after question. He still ignored me. "Fuck this shit! I'm getting out of here," I said reaching for the door handle. It was then that I realized there weren't any fucking door handles on the inside of the cab! "Fuck! What the fuck is going on?!" I screamed, pissed the fuck off. I knew Vincent was crazy but I didn't know he was this damn crazy! I guess I'm never going to be able to get away from his ass, now that he's kidnapping me. Wait, is it kidnapping when you're an adult? I guess it will be more so abducting me.

Vincent: Man where the fuck yo ass go?

Armani: like you don't already know!

Vincent: where are you dummy?! I'm tryna protect you!

That's when I realized that he wasn't talking to Vincent. Who in the hell was he talking to? "Who are you taking me to?" I asked him scared out of my mind. He still didn't answer me. He just continued to drive.

Armani: I flagged a cab down. Dis nigga crazy. No door handles so I can't get out. I heard him on the phone telling someone he's bringing me

Vincent: I told yo ass to come with me but you wanna sit there with that fuck boy!

Armani: Vincent plz help me

Vincent: it's too late

My eyes began to water up once I read his last message. I read it over and over, hoping the words would change but they never did. I began wrecking my brain trying to figure out who would want to abduct me. I had no fucking enemies because I had no friends. I only had Tamia and she would never hurt me. It had to be one of my sponsor's wives. Shit, if it is, I can beat her ass as soon as I can get out of this damn cab.

Armani: Dave. I've been abducted call 911

Dave: call Vincent bitch lose my number

Dave: Ima go fuck yo roommate!

I sat back stunned by his response to me needing his help. I told this man I'd been abducted and his ass told me he was going to fuck Tamia! What kind of shit is that? When I get out of this, Tamia is going to wish she was never fucking born.

We road in the cab for hours before it started to slow down and pulled into the yard of a nice home. He parked his cab in the garage and I knew I only had one more chance to let someone know what has happened to me. I log on to Facebook and post a status:

THIS IS NO JOKE! I'VE BEEN ABDUCTED SOMEONE CALL 911!!!

I posted the status and made sure my location was on so someone could find me. I slid my phone under the seat and heard it chime. I grabbed it and someone commented on my status saying **Girl you hell lol** and I had 12 likes! I mean, how much clearer can I be that this not a fucking joke! My phone made another noise indicating the battery is about to die. Fuck my life.

"You got her tied up?" I heard a man ask.

"Naw boss. I couldn't do all of that in public," the cabbie replied.

"I asked you to secure the bitch and get her here for $5,000 but you've only done half the job. I'm going into town, do the rest of your job and you know where to put her," the first guy said.

At this moment, I'm shitting bricks but I do know I have the advantage because I haven't been tied up and the cabbie isn't much bigger than me. I slid my phone under the seat after putting it on battery save mode. I become extremely quiet as I listen to what I assume is the first guy that was talking leaving in another car. I look back and I can see the shadow of the other guy pacing back and forth outside of the garage. Fuck, he's nervous! I thought I could take him but a scared man is a dangerous man. I've never fucked with anyone that was scared of me. The reason is because someone that's scared will fuck you up to keep you from fucking them up.

I heard the garage door opening and I laid back closing my eyes. I was going to pretend to be asleep until he came to the door. I could hear him inside of the garage with me but he sounded like he was pacing again. I started hearing noises and it sounded like he was going through some of the guy's things.

"Alright. The dumb bitch went to sleep, so I don't have to knock her ass out," he said and I didn't know if he had someone with him or if he was talking to himself. I had my body positioned leaning towards the middle so he would come around to grab my legs. "Let's do this!" he said hyped, letting me know he was alone.

The cabbie walked around to the side of the car and I waited a few seconds because I didn't know how close he was. I slowly lifted one eyelid taking a peek at him and he was so busy staring at my body that he didn't notice that I was looking dead at him. I waited for him to get closer to me before I closed my eyes back. As soon as I felt his hand touch my thigh, I started kicking him. He stumbled backwards into a wall of tools, knocking them off the shelves. Normally, I'd wait for a bitch to get up so we can fight straight up but this is a man and the odds are against me.

I run up on him kicking him in his stomach, trying hard as hell to break his ribs. He grabs one of my legs in mid kick pulling and spinning it, causing me to flip on my stomach. It happened so fast I didn't have time to use my hands to stop the impact of the fall. My chin hit the concrete garage floor and started bleeding. It felt like I bit my fucking tongue in half but I could still feel it throbbing. I lost a tooth though and that pissed me off! I'm going to kill this cabbie and everybody involved with this abduction! Then, I'm going back to fuck Tamia up for fucking with Dave.

"Look what you made me do, bitch!" the cabbie said getting up and breathing heavy. I had a mouth full of blood and spit at him. It hit his shoe, splattering on his pants leg. He reared back to kick me and I tried to stop his foot by catching it with my hands. The blow was so hard my hand went straight back causing me to yell out. There was no doubt in my mind that it was broken. He was relentless with his attack stomping me over and over.

"That's enough," I heard someone say just before everything went dark.

I woke up a few hours later with both hands tied together above my head. I looked up and noticed that my hand was still crooked. There was a rope tied to the rope that bind my hands together and it was tied to one of the bars on the headboard. My hand was broken and to keep from screaming out, I didn't try to break free.

I looked down the length of my naked bruised body and saw that my legs were tied to the bed posts at the foot of the bed. I started wondering what type of sick joke is this? Who does this to a person that has been through the amount of bullshit I've gone through in my life? I began to cry so hard that my body started rocking. My hand started hurting because I was moving it while I was crying. I looked down at my legs and I had bruises going all the way down my legs. It looked like someone took a hammer and hit me all over the front of my legs. It hurt to even move them as I cried. My head started hurting from all the crying I was doing. I was defeated, I hadn't done anything memorable with my life.

I began to think about my life to see what I will be remembered by. I came up blank. The only people that will remember are the wives of the men I've slept with. I'm sure they will be happy I'm gone, not knowing that just because it ain't me doesn't mean he's going to be faithful. There are plenty of bitches like me, willing to fuck a nigga for money married or not. I started thinking about Tamia, wondering if she was fucking Dave right now. I can't believe she would do this to me!

We have been through everything together, so she shouldn't do that to me. It's out of her character. I closed my eyes lost in thought.

"You missed me, baby girl?" I heard someone ask, causing me to look up.

"Steve?" I said just before passing out again.

Amere

It's been a few weeks since I've been able to have a conversation with Tamia and since seeing her, I've been missing her something terrible. All I've been thinking about is Tamia and the good times we had together. I miss having a chick that has something going for herself. She was always so positive. Every time I came home, there was a meal cooked and everything stayed cleaned. My only problem with her was that she put herself first, like it was only her. She never considered me in any decisions she made concerning her future. It was like she never saw a future with me to begin with.

Lisa has been getting on my last damn nerves! She finally finished furnishing the crib how she wants to and the shit is plain ugly. The living room is brown and yellow, the bathroom is green, and Armani's room is pink. I know it don't sound that bad but you have to see it for yourself. Every time I leave the house, she thinks I'm going to Tamia. She has no idea that Tamia ain't got her ass on me. Shit, I wish I was able to go to her whenever I wanted to. I'd always be over there kicking it with her. I wish like hell I could have been the man Tamia needed me to be when she gave me the chance. I fucked it up and now, I'm damn near stuck with this bitch that don't even compare.

I know where she lives and I found that out by accident. "Lisa, have you seen my wallet?" I yelled from our bedroom. I walked down the hall and she was sitting on the couch, and Amiria had toys all over the place. I just shook my head wondering if this how it would be if

I had a baby with Tamia. "Did you hear me?" I asked her.

"Naw, I haven't seen your wallet," she answered like I was getting on her nerves.

"Fuck," I said to myself.

I started looking all over the place for it because not only was my driver's license in it, but I had a very important number in it too. The other day I was in the projects they call *Dead Man's Zone* and ran into this dude name Duce. Duce was an ole crazy looking ass nigga and his left eye twitched. Anyway, I asked him about getting on, explained my situation to him, and he gave me this dude name Rashard's number. He kind of confused me because he said that Rashard is who I needed to talk to but he, himself, as in Duce, run these particular projects. If Duce ran the projects, then why did I need to talk to Rashard? Well, my phone was dead, so I wrote it down and stuck it in my wallet.

I'm going from room to room looking for my shit. I mean, I'm ransacking the place like the FEDs! "Maybe you left it at Tamia's house," Lisa said from the door. She was trying to be smart but I haven't been nowhere with Tamia's ass!

"Lisa, I haven't been with Tamia," I stated calmly.

"Well, who you been with?" she asked. I could tell she didn't have any information because she was fishing. Now, tell me what nigga gone tell on himself? I'm like Katt Williams, don't worry I'll wait. We all stand by the code lie, lie, lie and when you get caught, lie some more.

"Nobody Lisa, I been trying to find work," I answer her, getting aggravated. Then I thought about what she said and hopped in my car. I knew where I left my shit!

When I got to the stop sign, I pulled my phone out because I remember she told me no pop ups, ever since the first time we had sex. I didn't mind because I didn't want anyone knowing what was going on with us.

Amere: say baby girl. I think I left my wallet at yo place. Can I come through and look?

I pulled over at the gas station waiting on her to respond. It normally takes her five minutes, at the longest. Fifteen minutes later, I realized she was probably mad because I got a little carried away last time I was over there.

Amere: I'm sorry for laying hands on you. I need my wallet tho.

The bitch still didn't respond to me. I sat there thirty more minutes waiting on a reply that never came.

Amere: Armani man you foul af for not responding!

I know you sitting there reading thinking this nigga foul as fuck but you don't understand how shit happened. It was far from planned and Armani knows I only love Tamia, and she's ok with that. I fucked Armani for the first time years ago when Tamia first left me. That's when I kept going to Armani's door and she wouldn't let me in. Well, when she finally did, she wasn't acting like herself.

I walked in Armani's messy apartment with one thing on my mind and that was Tamia. "Where is she?" I asked Armani, who just sat across from me looking into space. She had me sitting there wondering what the hell she let me in for if she was going to ignore me when I got there. "Armani!" I yelled.

"What nigga? Why should I tell you? You didn't know what you had until you lost her and now, you want me to help you find her? For what? You should have loved her when you had the chance?" she screamed at me.

"I do love her and I'm going to come here every day until you tell me where she is," I said sincerely. I looked away waiting on her to snap but she didn't. When I looked back at her, her eyes were filled with tears. "What the hell is wrong with you?" I asked confused.

"I wish I had someone fight for me like you're fighting for her," she replied, plainly letting the tears fall. I ain't no fucked up ass nigga, so I got up and sat next to her. I put my arm around her and she laid on my chest. We stayed cuddled up until we fell asleep. I woke up and Armani was kissing on my neck. She started unbuckling my pants and I stopped her. "I just want to feel good," she said. Now, what kind of nigga would I be not to make her feel good when she's sitting here sad and I'm able to help?

I scooped her up in my arms, kicking shit out the way as I made my way to the first bedroom I came to. When I walked in, it was spotless so I knew it was

Tamia's bedroom. I wanted to take her to the other room but shit, we were in here now. "She's not coming back tonight," she stated as if reading my mind.

I allowed her to take my clothes off and she hopped on my dick. She was doing a piss poor job, so I began to guide her hips with my hands. It didn't take long for her to get the hang of it and before long, I was using my hands to slow her down. She came and I wasn't too far behind her. Afterwards, she walked me to the door and didn't mention it again.

We didn't fuck or communicate at all until that next year. She posted a picture on Facebook straddling a chair with all that ass hanging off. My dick got hard instantly. I started sending for her to come see me regularly. She never posted a status about Tamia and she never talked about her, so I assumed some shit popped off and they weren't friends anymore.

I didn't find out they were still close until she told me she lived alone, so I could come over to her place and it turned out to be a place she shared with Tamia. I got so fucking pissed off that I beat the fuck out of her. I had to beat her for all the pain this shit was going to cause Tamia when she found out. I knew she would find out eventually because Armani had been talking about us being exclusive, since I was the only dude she was fucking that wasn't married.

I didn't understand her logic at all. Why the fuck would I be exclusive with someone that was admitting to fucking married niggas. She was fucking us all for money. Shit, I'm really like Shy Glizzy that sing that shit that say "I can trust myself, I can't trust myself. So, the fuck I look like trusting anybody else?" Nigga had to have made the song for me because I promise you, I trust nobody!

I decide to just pop up on Tamia since Armani ain't responding. I'm really popping up on Armani but if Tamia answers, I'm going to act like I followed her home one day and have been trying to talk myself into knocking. I pull up to Tamia and Armani's building so I can get out but I see some dude with dreads coming out of the door. That's why the bitch wasn't answering! Her ass had one of them married men in there. Slutty ass bitch!

I wait until he gets in his car and he looks familiar, but I can't place it. After I watch him drive away, I head up to the door and knock. Tamia opens the door with a smile on her face that disappears as soon as she sees me. "What the hell Amere? What are you doing here?"

I stood there frozen, not really knowing what to say to her. I had all of these thoughts in my mind on the way over on how things would play out. I just knew when I saw her I would apologize and she would actually listen, and some kind of way we would be good. I stepped fully into the apartment and took a seat on the couch. The look on her face was priceless! I could tell she was shocked but I could tell she was pissed the fuck off too. "Is Armani here?" I asked her.

"No, I haven't seen her all day, why?" she returned.

"So, that nigga was here for you?" I asked, getting pissed off. The more I thought of someone else touching her body, the angrier I got. I couldn't believe she done came out here and turned into a hoe! Bitch was too focused to spend time with me but the way she opened the door smiling was like she feeling this nigga. She stood there with her arms folded across her chest and the meanest scowl I have ever seen on her pretty face. It was then that I realized I had never really seen her mad. I mean, I've seen her beat a few bitches up but she would fight at the drop of a dime. This scowl was towards me and I had never seen this side of her before. I didn't know what to expect.

She walked up slowly to me, swaying her hips with every step. She didn't close the door but I didn't care because I didn't want to break her stride. When she got within arm's length, I stood up to hold her but she reared back and slapped the fuck out of me.
"I been wanting to do that for years!" she said before sighing with relief. I was so damned confused. I didn't even say anything. I knew she felt like I deserved it.

"Can we talk?" I asked her.

"About?" she replied shortly.

"You and ole boy," I stated because I know she already knew.

"What about him? Before you answer that, remember you have no place in my life to question anything I have going on."

"You doing that shit Armani be doing?" I asked her and watched as she laughed. She laughed real hard then stopped out of nowhere.

"How you know what Armani does?" she asked with a straight face, like she wasn't just laughing a minute ago.

The question caught me off guard but being the nigga I am; I always think quick on my feet. "Shit, who don't know? You must still don't have a Facebook page?" I asked, changing the subject. She didn't respond. "Are you feeling him?" I asked her.

"Yes," she replied.

"Why?" I asked.

Rashard

I was so glad I hit Tamia up when I did because she is everything I assumed she would be. The only thing I wasn't thinking about is if she could cook or not. When I got to her house, I expected her to open the door with little shorts on and a tank top shirt, like most bitches do. Tamia had on sweatpants, a t-shirt that showed her stomach, and her hair was in a ball. The way some hair strands fell around her face made her appear angelic.

When I walked in, everything was clean. It made me wonder if she keeps everything like this or if she just did this on my way over here. I know some bitches shit be filthy and you won't know it unless you pop up on her. That or tell her you're on your way when you're not far enough away for her to actually clean up. Anyway, she gave me a quick tour opening and closing every door except one. I assume that's her roommate's room. When she opened the hall closet, I saw she had all of her towels folded in the same direction. She had all of the hangers facing the back of the closet and the blankets on the shelf. Yes, she a keeper!

We made it back to the living room and she turned on some show called *Revenge* that was on Netflix. I normally don't watch TV but it was a pretty good show. About ten minutes in though, I heard her stomach growl and she asked me if I wanted anything to eat. What nigga gone say no? I gave her a head nod and continued watching the show. I wanted to tell her to start the series completely over because I felt out of the loop and I liked to know everything.

We ate meatloaf, mashed potatoes with gravy, and sweet peas with some raspberry tea. The shit was bussing, I swear! I wanted to go in her room, pack up all her shit, and move her to my crib right now. After we ate, she took our plates in the kitchen but she didn't come right back. I don't trust people, so I got up to see what she was doing. She had a little grocery bag on the counter that she was dumping the remaining food off our plates into. I watch silently as she tied the bag and pressed down releasing all the air. She walked out the side door, placing the bag outside in the trashcan and came back in, cleaning our plates. She didn't sit them in the dish rack though, she dried them off with a paper towel and put them in the cabinet. I've never seen a woman my age do all of that. I walked back into the living room taking a seat on the couch.

A few minutes later, she came and joined me, apologizing for the wait. We talked about everything under the sun but I noticed she kept checking her phone and looking nervous. "What's the matter, Miss Lady?" I asked. She shook her head like nothing was wrong. I grabbed her chin turning her to me. "Listen, I'm here for you. Tell a nigga what's bothering you so I can help," I demanded.

"It's Armani, that's my roommate. She left this morning with one of her dudes and she hasn't been back a single time," she said. I thought it was cute that she was worried about her friend but if she was gone with a man, he probably decided to let her stay overnight.

"Maybe she stayed the night with the guy," I said and she gave me a strange look. I could tell she was trying not to tell me something. "You have to tell me everything babe." I don't know what made me call her that but I needed her to trust me. For some reason, since it was bothering her, it started to bother me too.

"Armani has four guys that she sleeps with for money. Three of them are married and I know nothing at all about the other one. He doesn't want anyone to know they mess around and she made sure she kept his secret, even from me. She left this morning with one of the married ones so she isn't staying the night," she paused as if thinking about something. I was glad she paused because I hadn't digested it all yet.

I was literally sitting here wondering if Tamia be doing the shit too. I mean, you are the company you keep, right? Instead of trying to help her, I was now trying to find a good exit. I felt like I was stuck between a rock and a hard place because she didn't seem like the type but she told me herself that her and ole girl was as thick as thieves.

When I looked back at her, she was looking at me with questioning eyes. "Look-," I started but she cut me off.

"I know you're thinking I do it too, which is why I didn't want to tell you. People are so quick to judge you off of someone else's actions. This an opposites attract type of friendship, not birds of a feather," she said and I released a breath I didn't even know I was holding. That caused both of us to burst out laughing.

"Finish telling me," I told her.

"Armani comes home periodically throughout the day," she said.

"How do you know?" I asked her. It's strange for her to know how often Armani is here when she's normally at school all day.

"I go to my first two classes and come back home for lunch. I clean up whatever it was that she left behind, eat, and go back. When I come back home between my last class and track practice, I have to clean again. Then after track practice but that late, it's normally just clothes," she said then started playing with her fingernails. I felt bad for her having to clean behind another grown woman.

I grabbed her hands into mine. "I'll find her for you," I said to her then leaned over kissing her forehead. She shifted her body so she could sit closer to me. I usually don't let bitches cuddle me but Tamia is going to be my wife. After a while I decided to leave, she looked disappointed but quickly smiled when she noticed I was looking at her. "I'm going to come see you when you get off work tomorrow, Miss Lady," I said kissing her forehead.

"What happened to babe? I kind of liked that," she said smiling.

"Come walk me out babe," I said to her before winking.

As soon as she opened the door, I saw a guy sitting in front of the building looking at the door. I didn't say anything to her; I just walked off heading towards my car. I was able to look at him without him knowing because he was still staring at the door. I had a bad feeling about what was about to happen and I had no clue what it was. I backed up so I can get a clear shot at his brake lights, so I could see if he had his foot on the brake or if he had the car in park. It was in park because the brake lights weren't on. That meant he was being patient, waiting on his time to enter.

I didn't know if he was there for Armani or Tamia, all I knew was Tamia was in there alone and she's unavailable. I hit a block and came back to park. Just as I expected, he was no longer in his car. I glanced up at the door and it was wide open, so I hopped out and walked casually to the door, standing in the foyer.

I listened to her ask him why he was there and he asked for Armani. I listened to their conversation until I heard a slap. I glanced around and she had done slapped fire from dude, and he sat back down. I don't place my hands on women in a violent way but I can't say I wouldn't start if one hit me like that. I continued listening until he started asking about me. I was making my way into the living room until he asked her if she was feeling me. I only stopped because I wanted to know how she felt. When she said yes, that was all I needed to hear to drop these bitches.

Man, I bet you never thought I'd be talking about dropping bitches! Shit, I'm normally trying to recruit these bitches to my team. Tamia's the perfect package though. She's what I've been subconsciously looking for. I started to send all my hoes a group message telling them it's over with, but I'll just ignore them and they'll get the point. "Why?" I heard this nigga say.

"Because I'm that nigga," I say, making my presence known. She turned towards me and winked before turning back around. That wink made ya boy want to scoop her little ass up and take her to her room to punish that pussy.

"This why you left the door open?" he asked, pointing to me.

"Why are you here?" I asked him before she could respond. I could see her with my peripheral vision shifting her weight from leg to leg, letting me know taking charge turns her on. Either she's turned on or she has to piss.

"Why nigga?" he asked looking at me. I could tell he had heart. If the circumstances were different, I'd give the nigga a job.

"This my girl," I said before glancing at Tamia, who was hiding her surprise very well. She didn't even look my way as she took a seat on the couch. "Who or what are you looking for?" I asked after noticing he kept looking towards the other bedroom. I began to put two and two together in my head. Some foul shit had been going on and I hate to hurt Tamia, but she's pretty blind to the bullshit.

"He's your ex, right babe?" I asked Tamia. She told me about him and described him and the chick he cheated on her with. Now that I think about it, this is the nigga that made Tamia run out the store at the mall. Man, I'd bet my last dollar that Armani was the chick following me at the mall!

"Yes," she answered me without looking away from the TV. I glanced at it and this crazy ass girl is watching *Revenge* again, like some shit ain't popping off right now in her damn living room! I'm telling you now, if you weren't listening before, dark skinned bitches are crazy!

I focused in on him, "Bruh, what's up? What do you need? How do you know where Tamia stay?" I asked him question after question. This nigga started sweating so I knew my assumption was right. I planned on hitting the blocks but shit looking like my girl will need me.

My last question must have caught Tamia's attention because she started mugging the fuck out of ole boy. "Yeen gone answer the question?" she asked him.

"I- I- I um… followed you home one day," he answered, looking at the wall behind her head. See, she probably thought he was looking directly at her but from the angle I'm standing, I can tell he ain't making eye contact. This nigga a real live liar! He knows he can't lie looking into her eyes, so he's focusing in behind her. I really should hire this nigga.

"Bullshit!" she replied standing up. I had no idea what she was about to do. You know these dark skinned bitches are unpredictable! I watched her get in a fighting stance like she's really about to bang dude out. "How you know where I live? Look at me nigga, not behind me," she said shocking the fuck out of me. I thought for sure her little ass was about to buy the shit.

He just stared at her. I stood there waiting on some shit to pop off so I can knock dude on his ass. She studied him, it looked like she was checking him out. If I weren't from the streets, I wouldn't know that she was sizing him up. I watched her face soften right before she started walking towards him. This is the smartest bitch I know and I need to marry her! She's literally using her fucking body to distract him. I've never been this excited in my life! As soon as she got close to him, she closed her eyes and stood on the tips of her toes. Once he closed his eyes, she struck his ass! She hit buddy so damn hard, he stumbled backwards. She ain't let up though. Tamia two pieced his ass all the way up against the wall.

It took him a minute but once he got his bearings together, he cocked back about to hit her. I hopped over the couch coming down on the top of his head with all my might, elbow first. When I stood up, Tamia was sitting back on the couch about to press play on that damn show! "Is he dead?" she asked without looking back. That's when I realized, he hadn't got up or moved.

"Come check his pulse," I told her.

She ignored me and started back watching the show. Tamia doesn't know it but she's going to learn how to mind me. I walked around the couch and stood in front of her. She glared up at me. "Go check his pulse," I told her calmly. She rolled her eyes but she got up and went to do as she was told.

"It's still there," she said walking into the kitchen. I had no idea what she was doing until she came back out with a cooler. Her cock strong ass lifts it up, pouring it all over buddy. He jumped up screaming. "Get the fuck out my house, nigga," she said with one hand pointing towards the door and the other one on her hip. I could tell he was pissed off but what my lady said goes.

After he left, she locked the door then cleaned up the mess she made on the floor. Once she came back to the couch, she wasn't looking like a thing happened. "Are you ok, Miss Lady?" I asked because I don't want her holding anything in.

"No," she replied clicking play. I could tell that watching Netflix was her way of escaping pain. Most people go to drugs, writing, cleaning, exercising, and acting out. I'm glad her outlet was simple because I would hate to be around when something pop off and she forgot her Netflix password.

Michelle

It's been a week since I've been released from the hospital and Ray hasn't come by to check on me. I know he's heard about it by now, so why hasn't he came by? I know he doesn't have my new number but my address is still the same. I miss him so much! I'll never leave him alone, no matter what because I love him so much.

I didn't realize how much I loved him until I thought he was dead. Tiffany told me he was very much alive and that she saw him at the mall the day after I was hospitalized. I asked her if she told him where I was and she hesitated then said yes, so I knew she was lying. She knows all of our problems so she naturally wants me to leave him alone. If I could I would, but I can't so I ain't! Petty? So fucking what, it's my life. One day, Ray will be done with them hoes and he's going to come back to me, so we can make a family. I know he talks to other bitches but them hoes can't beat our history. Ray loves me and I can tell because he comes to see me every week. He's a pretty busy dude so that's a big deal!

Tiffany: What's good bitch wyd

Michelle: chillin whats up???

Tiffany: it's Deuce bday and Carte Blanche

opened back up yesterday

Michelle: and?

Tiffany: and bitch dey having his bday bash there ya boy throwin it hoe!

Michelle: okay! Bitch we gotta hit the mall

I was so excited to dress up for Ray! We haven't been out together in so long. I wish I knew what colors he was going to wear, so we could color coordinate.

Tiffany: omw

After I read the last text from Tiffany, I know I have to hurry up. I haven't seen Ray in a while, so I need to make sure I give my man a night to remember. After a quick shower, I throw on some jeans and a graphic tee. I have natural short hair so I wet it and wait for Tiffany to arrive.

I heard Tiffany knocking on my door using the grindin beat from back in the day. I swung the door open, stepping out before she came in. If I would have let her come in, I'd have to wait for her to find something to eat and eat it before we would be ready to go. We pulled up to *Devonshire Mall* and hopped out on a mission. "What are you going to wear?" Tiffany asked me.

"I'm thinking something classy for Ray. I'm going to wear black so it will match whatever he's wearing for pictures," I said to her. She looked at me strangely with a smirk on her face. I'm really tired of her not allowing me to live my life the way I want to without judgment! Every time I turn around it's, "you need to leave him alone" or "girl you need to know your worth"! I get so tired of hearing those cliché ass speeches!

See, y'all don't know or understand the type of man Ray is. When you love someone, you will move every mountain for them, walk across water for them so waiting for them to get it right should be the easiest, right? Like I said before, what man sits at a female's house every week hanging out that's he's been with on and off for six years? We still have sex and I do his hair for him because he knows I don't want anyone else in it!

As we're walking through the mall, I catch a familiar face walking into *Aeropostale*. "Hey, I think that's Tamia from the hospital," I say to Tiffany.

"Go chase after ya master then puppy," Tiffany said, rolling her eyes. Tiffany made it clear that she didn't like her but she had no logical reason. They have never messed with the same guy as far as Tiffany knows and they have never bumped heads before. When I asked Tiffany why she didn't like her, she said it's because Tamia thought her shit didn't stink. She didn't seem to be that type of person to me though. She seemed pretty cool and down to earth.

I walked in the store behind her. I was about to approach her to speak but I thought about how I looked like a stalker. She was shadowing my nurse for some of the days I was in the hospital and here I am, chasing her down to speak like we are long lost friends. I guess it's just that she seemed so cool at the hospital and as weird as it may sound, I kind of admired her. We are the same age but she seems to have it so put together.

"Can I hang a poster in here please, Ms. Kathy?" I heard Tamia ask the store clerk, snapping me back to reality. Either she shops here a lot or she's that bitch that everybody likes! Well except Tiffany, but she has no valid reason.

"Sure thing. Come on and let me show you where to put it," the store clerk said coming from around the counter.

"Hey, how are you?" she stopped and asked me before she passed me. She made me feel so special because I can see that she's clearly busy but she made time to see how I'm doing.

"Much better, thank you," I replied.

"That's good," she said, walking away and following the clerk to the front of the store. I browsed around the store as she put the poster up so it wouldn't look like I was stalking her. I also wanted to see what was on it. As if she was reading my mind, she walked up to me "Hold on to this for me and if you see her, call me," she said. It was then that I saw the sadness behind her eyes.

"Are you ok?" I asked her.

"Yes I am. Well, I will be as soon as I find her. She was my best friend," she replied like the girl was dead. It literally sounded like she has lost hope and just wanted to have a funeral.

"She may still be alive. What happened?" I asked.

"Well, she won't be after I make sure she's safe. She was abducted almost two weeks ago. She asked two guys for help and they refused. She posted a Facebook status telling people what was happening to her but everyone thought she was joking," She rambled off.

"What?! Who plays like that and why didn't she call you?" I asked, getting pissed off that she could have been saved had someone tried to help her. I can only imagine what she's going through right now.

"I'm going to make sure I ask her when I find her. Well, it was nice talking to you but I have to get going," she said turning to leave.

"Um… wait! Tamia, can I get your number? You know, to keep in touch," I asked nervously. I'm not gay but it felt like I was asking her out on a date. She's the kind of friend everyone needs. I wonder what this girl did to her for her to call her, her best friend in past tense.

"It's on the flyer, Michelle," she said before walking out of the store. I stood there in awe because she remembered my name. When she didn't say it at first, I kind of assumed she forgot it. I would have understood because Detroit Medical is the busiest hospital we have.

I went to catch up with Tiffany. I knew she was at the food court because she's greedy as hell. She was eating one of those big ass pretzels looking like she was high. "What are you wearing?" I asked her.
"I don't know, let's go to *Rainbow* and see what they have," she suggested. I followed behind her but all of a sudden, I wasn't feeling *Rainbow*.

I was thinking about Tamia and what she would wear if she would go, and I didn't think it would be anything out of *Rainbow*. Plus, I needed to fix Ray and my relationship, and I know he would want me on point. "Chelle? Is that you?" I heard a voice say. I turned around and it was Candy from *Carte Blanche*.

"Hey Candy! How you been?" I asked her.

"Fuck all that bitch, where you been? Raphael been looking for you. Rashard stopped by looking for you! Your ass has been missing in action!" she said. The only thing I heard was Rashard was looking for me. See, I told y'all Ray loved me! He didn't have my new number but he was popping up at my job looking for me. That's when it hit me that I haven't talked to Raphael yet about work!

"Girl, almost 2 weeks ago, I was heading into work. I was late but I was coming. Anyway, people were shooting! A bullet went through my car and me!" I told her.

"No!" she yelled, covering her mouth. Her eyes began to water like she was about to cry.

"Don't worry, I'm ok now. I hopped out of my car once the police got there and saw Ray's car flipping, and it blew up! Girl, I thought he was dead and every time I asked about him at the hospital,
they kept telling me they had no record of him being there!" I said in one breath.

"Well, he's very much alive and throwing a party tonight for his homeboy. You want to work it? It's going to be hella money involved," she said to me.

Now, don't get me wrong. I love the fuck out of Ray but if I have to choose between following him around like a lost puppy and making money, then money will win every time! "Hell yeah! Count me in! Now I don't have to buy an outfit," I said as we both laughed.

"Come at 7 tonight because the doors open at 9. He wants everyone's hair long tonight. Can you make that happen?" she asked as I nodded my head. "Well, it was good seeing you and I'm glad you're ok," she said while walking away.

I walked in Rainbow to find Tiffany looking through the clearance rack. She was about to get about four dresses for less than $30. That's how Rainbow worked. "Bitch, I'm working the party tonight," I walked up telling Tiffany. She looked at me and smiled but continued to look through the clothing rack. After she purchased her stuff, we headed back to my place so we could start getting ready.

I washed my hair then blow dried it and sat down so, Tiffany could braid it for me. I always got Tiffany to braid my hair when I was doing my sew ins because I could never get my own sew in tight enough. About two hours later, I now had twenty-three inches of Brazilian hair and you couldn't tell me nothing! Tiffany just wanted a wash and set. She decided to ride with me so she wouldn't miss out on anything. I don't know what she meant by that.

We were both dressed and ready looking bad as fuck, especially me with this long ass hair! We walked in about 6:30 so I could see if there was anything I needed to do before 7. When I found Raphael, he stood up to greet me. He gave me a tight hug, so I know Candy told him what happened to me. "Anything you need me to do?" I asked.

"Naw, Tamia seems to have it covered. I'll let her know you're willing to help if she needs you," he responded.

I stood there staring at him wondering if he's talking about my friend, Tamia. She would have told me if she worked here, right? I walked out of Raphael's office in search of Tamia. When I found her, she was telling the DJ where she wants him. She was moving him from his normal spot and I didn't want Raphael to say anything to her. "Tamia, hey, excuse me. Raphael normally wants our DJ over in that corner," I said with a smile.

"Hey Michelle. Do you work here?" she asked looking at me suspiciously.

"Yes. I'm not following you," I said causing us both to laugh. I think she thought I was following her for real because she was cracking up! At first, I was a little offended that she didn't tell me she was going to be working here, but now I see employment hasn't come up yet because she didn't know I worked here either.

"Oh ok. Well, I'm going to have the photo booth set up where y'all normally have your DJ because the lighting is better. The sound carries more from this corner, so I'm setting up the stage and the DJ here. Raphael knows already, he said do me, but put everything back when I'm done," she said.

"Oh! You know Raphael? I'm just wondering what are you doing here?" I asked her.

"I'm the host for Deuce's birthday bash tonight. I don't normally do things like this but the money is awesome, and I had a free day today," she said with a smile. I smiled back and walked off. I wonder why they hired her instead of just letting Candy do what she normally did. Something isn't right and I'm going to find out what it is.

Tiffany

Ha! I know y'all been waiting on a bitch like me to speak up, but I sometimes prefer to move in silence. You will never see or hear me coming! In case you didn't know, I'm Tiffany Smith, Michelle's cousin and Rashard's little side piece. Before you judge me, think about it for a second. Don't sit there and act like you've never been the side chick. Hell, we all have been there, whether we know it or not because you will never meet a nigga that ain't fucking somebody! So just so you know, asking him if he's in a relationship is the wrong question. Niggas don't care these days anyway. If you play your cards right, eventually you will move into the main slot.

I've been messing with Shard's fine ass for about four years. At first, he was all up Michelle's ass and no bitch, and I do mean no bitch, could take him from her. She would always brag about his dick and how he was doing this, that and the other for her and just being honest, I wanted it for myself. I'm the prime example of why you don't tell a lonely bitch your happy stories.

When she got pregnant by him, everything went from glitter to shit. He started fucking everybody! He still wouldn't fuck me though, but I had a trick for his ass. It had been four weeks since I had my second child, meaning my girl was ready to get fucked! Well, I thought she was. I had no idea some people experience dryness right after having a baby. Anyway, I threw a little spades party, making sure to invite enough people for Shard to actually come through.

While we were playing spades, I brought the liquor out. My home girl, Trina, kept asking where my kids were, trying to be funny. Nobody had to worry about them because I gave them both a nice dose of Benadryl about ten minutes before everybody started showing up. Anyway, I spent most of my time in the kitchen mixing drinks, trying to get Shard too fucked up to drive home.

I noticed he would down a shot and a few minutes later, he would be drinking water or eating. This nigga was too fucking smart! The water or bread wouldn't help him with this roofie though! Man, I kept Rohypnol on deck because I be trying to trap a baller! I dropped it in his shot and took it to him along with a bottle of water. He grabbed the shot and downed it. I waited a few minutes until it started kicking in. They kicked him out of the spades game because he was fucking his partner up. I helped him to my room and went to clear up the party. "Where my boy at?" Dre asked while I was cleaning up.

"He wants to sleep a bit of the shit off. I'll call you when he's ready," I answered. He gave me a head nod before leaving. I didn't want him to sleep too hard so I would have to clean up after we finished. I walked in my room and removed his shoes and jeans. Shard's ass was dead to the world until I wrapped my mouth around that big ole dick of his.

He started moaning as I bobbed my head up and down the shaft of his dick while cupping his balls in my hands. It wasn't long before he grabbed my hair and started fucking my mouth. No nigga can out fuck me, so I tightened my jaws muscles and he slowed his pace. I took him deeper and deeper until he released down my throat. Mission accomplished!

I stood up to walk into the living room, so I could clean up. I turned the music back on so I could jam while I cleaned. "Who the fuck told you we were done?" Shard said, coming up behind me. He slapped my ass, grabbing a handful of it before smacking it again. I stood up, turned around, and he already had a condom on! I tried walking pass him back into the room but he grabbed my arm, bending me over the couch. He pulled my shorts and underwear off, and I couldn't wait to feel him inside of me. He had a little trouble because of his size and I had just had a baby, so it felt like I was a virgin again. It was painful but it was good too.

Neither one of us got a chance to cum because after about only a few minutes, he pulled out and took the condom off. I looked back at him because if he wanted to go in raw, that was fine with me. "Get on your knees," he said. I happily obliged, taking him back in my mouth. I rotated from sucking the head to gently licking his balls while jacking him off. I deep throated him over and over until he pulled out, nutting all over my face. It pissed me off but I didn't say a thing.

I been sucking him off ever since. It wasn't until I tried to have sex with again that he told me my shit was dry as fuck. He just caught me at a bad time because I've never had any complaints in that department. I'm a real bad bitch too, redbone and thick as fuck! His ass still will only let me suck his dick, but that's enough for me. I can swing through, suck the nigga's soul through his dick, and then go get fucked by someone else! It's a win, win situation.

Anyway, Shard hasn't been answering any calls or texts since our last time together. I don't know if he told you or not, but I sucked his dick and waited until he fell asleep to try and fuck him, and he kicked my ass out! Man, I was so mad and embarrassed. I love his ass and I need him to give us a real shot! We will be good together. I only have five kids now and they can go live with my mama, so me and Shard can be happy together.

Ever since he hadn't been answering me, I've been following him. At first, he wasn't really fucking with nobody, but I knew soon he would be back at Michelle house fucking her! She told me he came once a week spending time with her and fucking her, so I had to get her out of the picture!

I linked up with Brittany, the bartender at the bar and grille that Michelle works at to get Michelle's schedule. When Brittany texted me that Wednesday night to let me know Michelle works on Friday, we set plan "Get Michelle out the way" in motion. We talked to Brittany's brother and a few of his friends, letting them know to grab Michelle and do whatever they wanted with her, then handle my issue. I lied like I would pay them fifty grand a piece. It was four of them, Brittany told them about Rashard being in the VIP Booth and how Raphael would be watching Michelle.

I totally forgot to give them a picture of her, so I had no idea if they knew who their target was or not. I also didn't count on them running their mouths like some bitches! I heard around the way that the jump boys were going to roll up on them after they left the club and get the money I lied about paying them! It's a good thing none of their asses survived! Now, I have to find Brittany because she's the only one that can tie me to the shit. I've been so determined to get that main spot that I'll do anything. Once you get a dose of Shard, I bet you will understand where I'm coming from!

I noticed that he started making himself friendly with that bitch, Tamia. She walks around with this holier than thou attitude, like she has done no wrong. She thinks she's the shit because she's in school and about to graduate, but the bitch still ain't shit! So now on top of Michelle, I got to compete with this bitch too! That's why I don't like her but hell, I couldn't tell Michelle that when she asked me about it.

Lately, Shard and Tamia been kicking it heavy! This nigga is at her house every night after she leaves work. I know this because I follow him around all day while texting him. He never responds though, which is really pissing me the fuck off! Anyway, when he pulls up to her house, she always opens the door in scrubs. He doesn't even give her time to wash her ass before he's over there.

When I found out she was going to be hosting Deuce's birthday party tonight, I figured what better way than to kill two birds with one stone! That's when I decided to invite Michelle out. It made it even better when she volunteered to work the party. I knew with both of them working, they would clash! I also knew from watching Shard that he was going to be wherever Tamia was. I didn't want to miss a moment of it. When I let the shit slip, I was so glad Michelle's dumb ass didn't catch it.

Anyway, we get to the bar and it's pretty much empty, which should be expected this early. We walk in together but go our separate ways. I sat in the back corner, so I could watch everything and wouldn't be seen easily. Watching Tamia give orders made my ass itch! I wanted to get up and trip her so she would break her pretty front teeth. I swear I can't stand bitches like her.

After Michelle went to her boss' office, she came out heading straight for Tamia with a confused look on her that was far too funny. She was probably wondering what the hell Tamia was doing there. After several minutes, she walked away looking at the floor. She must be disappointed.

Around 8:30, all the hoes started flocking in and trust me baby when I say they're choosing! I was looking everywhere for Shard but I couldn't find him. I chalked it up to him being with the birthday boy. I noticed Michelle was really working the crowd with her long hair. My cousin was on point tonight! Hopefully, she got her own man because Rashard was mine from the moment he stuck his dick in my mouth.

"Excuse ma'am. Can I buy you a drink?" Some young dude walked up asking me. First of all, I'm not old so why the fuck is this little ass nigga calling me ma'am.

"How many can you afford?" I asked him.

"What you mean?" he asked.

"Let me see what's in your pocket," I said with my hand out.

"Bitch, is we fucking after this?" he asked rudely. See, this little ass boy got me fucked up.

I stood up but before I could react, Michelle brought her extra skinny ass to the table. "Lil June, leave my cousin alone before she slaps you," she said, sliding in between him and me.

"She slap me, I'ma fuck her fine thick ass," he said, licking his lips while looking around her at me. See, this nigga gone make me catch a charge with his young ass.

"How old are?" I asked him.

"Eighteen," he responded, causing me to roll my eyes. I sat back down because I am not about to waste my time with this boy fresh out of high school.

June walked away and I noticed a little bit of commotion at the entrance. "Everybody get up and put ya hands together for da birthday boy, DEUCE!" Tamia said over the microphone all excited and shit. If I didn't know any better, I'd think she was fucking him too! Rashard walked in right behind him and winked at

Tamia. When I looked at her, she was blushing! Black ass bitch!

"Let me go speak to Ray," Michelle's gullible ass said before walking off. She didn't wait to see if I was coming or not, so I sat back watching to see how everything would play out. She walked right up to him, arms extended and I glanced at Tamia who was watching Rashard like a hawk! I was so excited. I was sitting at my table smiling from ear to ear. He stepped to the side and whispered something in her ear. She turned around and he pointed at Tamia, and Michelle took off running. He swaggered his sexy ass right on up to Tamia and kissed her on the lips.

"Enjoy the show?" I heard from behind me. I turned to look and it was the stripper bitch, Candy.

"What?" I asked playing dumb.

"Bitch, don't play dumb with me. Any real friend wouldn't have let her run off like that without going to check on her, and you're her damn cousin. I see ya trifling ass sitting here watching Rashard," Candy said to me. If I could fight, I would beat the fuck out of her right now for coming out the side of her neck like that.

"I was just about to go check on her," I said getting up and walking in the direction Michelle ran off to.

Tamia

Rashard and I have been spending so much time together. He's already ready for me to meet his family but I'm not sure about that right now. The police still don't have any leads on Armani and I'm extremely worried about her. I was mad at her for the foul shit her and Amere been doing behind my back, but I didn't stop caring about her well-being.

I didn't find out about them until the day he popped up at my house. It took Rashard asking him questions for me to wonder the same thing. When I looked down at his feet, he had on smoke gray Timberland boots and that was all the confirmation I needed. Remember when I woke up cooking in the middle of night and tripped over a dark gray boot, right? Remember I was sitting on the couch and I heard someone say oh shit, but when I turned around, nobody was there?

See, I thought I was tripping that night but now that I have more information, I know what's been going on. Armani told me everything about all her sponsors except him. I guess when they first started talking he was flying her back home. I have no idea how she got him in here without me knowing it! I guess I don't pay enough attention to my surroundings. One thing I do remember though is those boots! Now I know why she wouldn't tell me about him! Rashard told me he thinks that Amere may have left something here and that's why he popped up.

As trifling as Armani is though, I still want to make sure she's ok. Once I get her back here, I plan on beating the dog shit out of her and moving out. She can continue to be Amere's side chick all she wants because he isn't my problem anymore. I only slapped him because he claims to want me back, yet he's been sleeping with Armani!

Anyway, Rashard knows how worried I am about her, so he comes over every day to keep my mind off her. I tried calling her but her phone is dead, and the police can't locate it. I just hope nothing detrimental is happening to her because she's already been through so much.

Rashard told me he's been putting his ear to the streets but it's only so much he can do. I understand he knows a lot of people but none of those people matter if the person that took her doesn't know them.

He had been asking me for a few days now to host his homeboy, Deuce's Birthday Bash at a club he said he rented out. The only reason I agreed is because it will give me something else to focus on besides Armani. I'm still wondering daily why she didn't reach out to me in her time of need! The police pulled her phone record and saw she reached out to two men and even Facebook, and no one bothered to help her.

Anyway, I have to get down to the club to see what I'm working with. I've never hosted anything before, so I hope it's as easy as Rashard was making it seem.

When I walked in the club, it was really nice inside. It looked like a hole in the wall from the outside but it's spacious in here. The bar is the closest thing to the door which is good because it alluring. The chick they have working it right now will not be working it the night of the party. I'm thinking of a hood classy party. I know all these niggas like a little bit of ratchetness, but they love class. Women that know how to carry themselves in public with grace are winning! Do what you want behind closed doors but men respect women that respect themselves.

"Hey baby," Rashard said, walking up behind me and wrapping his arms around my waist.

"Trying to see what I'm going to do to spruce this place up for the party," I said stepping out of his embrace. I looked up at his handsome angry face with his dreads neatly braided straight back and smiled. "Not much is wrong here but this place is missing a lady's touch. For the night, I'm in charge, ok?" I asked before standing on the tips of my toes to kiss his lips.

"C'mon crazy ass girl, let me introduce you to Candy," he said, grabbing my hand. I began to wonder if Candy is her real name or stripper name. Not many people name their children job appropriate names these days, so I wouldn't be surprised if it was. Now before you get offended, put yourself in a boss' position. Now imagine what type of business you're in if you will hire a 'Candy'. Now do you get my point?

We walked in a nice office and I could see Candy was in deep thought reading over some paperwork on the desk. Rashard cleared his throat causing her to look up with the brightest smile I've seen in I don't know how long. She stood up giving Rashard a half hug then walked over to me, hugging me as well. "I'm Candy," she said smiling but I was too lost in her aura to respond.

She had this presence about her that I had never been in the company of. Most females aren't like this. She is indeed a rare breed. Hell, even I was judging her by her name before I ever met her and that's what females do. It doesn't matter what your name is, a female somewhere is going to comment on it. It's either your parents are ghetto or they think they're white. Once you get past that, they will mentally judge you based on what you're wearing and how you carry yourself. Not Candy though, she exuded so much confidence! I could tell right off the back how strong she is.

Rashard nudged my arm, jarring me out of my thoughts. "Oh, I'm sorry, I'm Tamia. I was a little lost in my own thoughts," I said apologizing for being rude.

"It's ok," Candy replied taking a seat.

"Well, I was coming in here to introduce y'all but Candy took over," Rashard said causing us all to laugh. "Well, Tamia is going to host the party and she's doing a little make over, so let Raphael know what's up. I have to go," Rashard said before kissing my forehead and walking away.

"I'll be right back, let me go tell Raphael what he said," Candy said standing to her feet.

"I'm coming with you," I responded, allowing her to lead the way. I followed her to the bar as she took a seat next to who I assume is Raphael.

"What's up Candy?" Raphael asked without bothering to look behind him where I was standing.

"Shard said Tamia will be hosting the party tonight. Whatever she says goes, cool?" she said to him.

He turned around slowly looking me up and down. "You Tamia?" he asked.

"Yes," I responded with a smile. I glanced at Candy and she was smiling too.

"Well do you, just put everything back when you're done," he said before turning back around.

"Will do," I said walking away.

Now it's time to get started on bringing this club to life! I mean it's fine the way it is, but not if I'm going to host a party here. I set speakers up in each corner to see where it sounded the loudest from the dance floor. I figured if the people barely heard the music they'd spend more time talking than dancing. I couldn't have that at a party I was hosting.

"Excuse me. I'm Tamia, what are your names?" I asked approaching two guys that were standing by the bar. They had *Security* on the back of their shirts, so I decided to ask them to help me out a bit.

"Tony," the taller, darker one answered.

"Roy," replied the other one. "What can I do for you, ma'am? The club doesn't open for a while," Roy said to me like I was aggravating him. If me approaching them bothered him, then wait until I put them to work!

"I need the speakers and stage moved to this corner over here," I said, pointing to the corner I wanted them moved to.

"Ma'am, the boss doesn't like when things are moved," Roy said to me. I could already tell that he was going to have a problem taking orders from a woman.

It's nothing he had to get used to, hell, I'm only here for one night.

"Roy, I wouldn't come over here asking for help if I had not already spoken to Raphael. It's a go sweetie, so can we get this done before the club opens?" I asked plainly with a serious face.

Roy walked away without saying a word to me heading in the direction of Raphael's office. "I'm sorry Tamia, Roy just doesn't like females ordering him around. You should see how he does Candy," Tony said apologizing for Roy's behavior. Something he said about Candy caught my attention. Rashard made it seem like she was just a dancer here, but it seems like Ms. Candy got clout!

"It's ok, Tony. I only have to deal with him tonight," I replied with a smile. I watched Roy storm out of Raphael's office heading back in our direction. I reached for my purse but forgot I left it in my car. I needed to get my brass knuckles out if I was going to have to fight this big ass nigga! I knew he'd kick my ass either way but with my brass knuckles, I could do some damage. I could leave his big ass something to remember me by.

"Let's get to work!" he yelled, taking his frustrations out on Tony. Tony didn't reply; he just walked away. I stood around directing them on where to put each speaker. I had the stage slightly out of the corner with the DJ Booth sitting on the back left hand side of the stage. I got Roy to bring the small refrigerator out of the office and plug it in behind the DJ Booth. I already had bottled water in my car, so I went out and brought in 6 bottles for the DJ. He smiled and thanked me. It wasn't until he told me that he normally doesn't get anything like this that I realized why he seemed so appreciative. I don't know what kind of business Raphael is running if he ain't taking care of his employees.

I had Roy to turn all four speakers diagonally towards the dance floor. Once I got the stage, speakers, and DJ Booth how I wanted it, it was time for a sound test. I grabbed the mic and stood in the middle of the dance floor. "Mic check 1, 2. Mic check 1, 2," I said into the microphone. I walked through each part of the club repeating the same phrase. I got Candy to take me up to the VIP Booths because I didn't have security access to get to them. Candy loved how everything sounded this way. As strange as it may seem, I felt good knowing I had pleased her, especially with this being my first time.

"You're doing awesome, Tamia," Candy said to me.

"Thanks girl. I been working the fuck out of Roy for getting an attitude with me though," I said causing her to laugh.

"Girl, I do the same shit! You would think he'd be used to taking orders from a boss bitch cause I stay on his ass!" she said to me.

"So, what do you do here?" I asked her as we descended to the dance floor.

"I'm a dancer, host, and I'm over the bar and security," she answered me.

"Wow. You're a jack of all trades, huh?" I said to her as she nodded and laughed again.

"Well, let me finish up and I'll come chat with you in a bit," I said to Candy as I walked away. As lonely as I be, I hope we can build a friendship after this. Armani is ok and all, but we can't ever have a conversation without arguing anymore. Now that she's missing, I miss cleaning up behind her and fussing about dumb stuff. I really hope she's ok.

I stood back for a second trying to figure out what I wanted to do with this place next when I felt my phone buzz in my pocket.

Amere: Tamia I really am sorry.

Tamia: I know.

Amere: Can I see you?

Tamia: No

Amere: Why not?

Amere: cuz u wit dat nigga?!!!

I slid my phone in my pocket because this nigga has some nerve! How the fuck he gone cheat on me when we were together, have a baby on me, fuck my best friend and then try to get back with me? I swear I don't understand the logic behind some people's thinking.

Rashard: how's it going beautiful?

Tamia: everything is everything

Rashard: whats wrong miss lady?

Tamia: nothing

Rashard: I'll be there in a few minutes.

I have no idea how Rashard always knows when something is bothering me. I'm normally pretty good at hiding how I feel but his ass really sees right through the bullshit!

Instead of standing around mad at the nerve of a nigga I'm never going to be with again, I decide to finish working. I look around and notice some of the girls that work here are arriving. I'm glad too because I had no idea what they looked like. I walked up to a skinny, dark skin chick checking her out. She had on a loose fitting tank top shirt with some black shorts that said *Carte Blanche* on the back of them. How tacky is that shit? I looked around and noticed the other girls had on the same thing. "Excuse me, I'm Tamia. What's your name?" I asked the chick I was checking out.

"Goldie," she responded dryly and my mouth dropped. I watched her walk away, like no this extra black ass bitch doesn't call herself Goldie! What's really going on here?

I don't know how long I was standing there but Candy approached me, giggling and snapping me out of my trance. "What did she say to you?" Candy asked.

"Now Candy, y'all know y'all wrong for calling that bitch Goldie!" I said as Candy cracked up with laughter. She was in tears, bending over and everything. I'm standing here looking crazy because I didn't see a damn thing funny about this bitch who is as dark as *Blade* calling herself Goldie!

"Come on girl. Let me introduce you to the girls," she said still chuckling. As we walked into the dressing room, I was surprised it looked nice. Candy and I walked to the front of the room, and I waited as she cleared her throat.

"Is she a new girl?" *Blade,* I mean Goldie asked causing Candy to glare at her. Goldie completely ignored her as she gave me the once over.

"Listen up ladies! This is Tamia and she will be hosting Deuce's Party tonight. Raphael has given her free reign, so what she says goes. I'm sure she won't make you do anything you aren't comfortable with. If she tells you to do something you don't want to do, don't come to me because I respect her judgement. I'm going to back her decisions. Are we crystal?" Candy asked.

"Clear," the girls said in unison.

"Good. Tamia, the floor is yours," Candy said to me then took a step back.

I've never been so nervous in my life. Here I am standing in front of five girls waiting on me to give orders that I haven't thought of yet. "I'd like for you to stand, state your name, and spin slowly for me one at a time," I spoke clearly.

"The fuck is this, an Uncle Luke video audition or something?" Goldie asked.

"Do it or take your extraterrestrial black ass home! I'm female but ain't no bitch in my blood sweetie, so please don't let the size fool ya!" I snapped on her. See with bitches like her, you have to nip that shit in the bud quick before her attitude spread like wildfire and all these bitches will be talking crazy.

She didn't respond which was a good thing. She stood up. "I'm Goldie," she said and turned around slowly. She was skinny, dark skinned, and her hair looked like it needed to be washed. She had it in a ponytail like she doesn't work at a fucking club! She had small breasts and no ass, and it had me wondering how she got this job anyway.

"What do you do here?" I asked her.

"I'm a server," she replied. I personally would only hire eye candy and Goldie was far from it. Don't get me wrong, she had a cute face but you should have more than that to work at a club!

"Is there a shower in here?" I turned whispering to Candy and she nodded her head. "Shampoo and conditioner?" I asked and she nodded her head. "Goldie, I need you to go hop in the shower and wash your hair really good. Don't put it back in a ponytail please," I said, turning back around to face the group. She stormed out as a brown skinned chick giggled. I shot a cold glare at her stopping her from laughing.

"Next," I responded, gesturing for the next girl to stand up.

"I'm Tammy," she said standing up and doing a slow spin. Tammy is the eye candy you need waitressing tables! She's light skinned with a big bubble butt and shoulder length hair. She has small breasts and gray eyes. She could get so many tips if she were a waitress with those eyes alone!

"What do you do here?" I asked her.

"I'm a cage dancer," she replied, throwing me for a loop. I made a mental note to ask Candy about that later. They didn't know it yet but nobody would be dancing in cages tonight. I needed all these ladies mingling with the fellas tonight.

"Next," I said to the chick seated next to her.

"I'm Ashley," she said standing and doing a slow spin. Ashley is a brown skinned cutie. All of these ladies are cute; they just aren't in the right positions to make money. Ashley has really big breasts but no ass at all. She was thick though and I knew the perfect position for her tonight. She had a choppy hair cut that looked more like an accident than a style. I hope she didn't pay for it.

"What do you do here?" I asked her.

"I'm a server," she replied smiling. I'm like, really bitch? I wanted to know about her tips because I don't see a nigga tipping when the bitch ain't got no ass!

"Next," I said.

"I'm Tia and I'm a cage dancer," Tia said doing a slow spin before taking her seat.

"I'm Megan and I'm a bartender," she stood up saying while following suit. I didn't mind at all because it sped up the process, so I could move on to my next plan of action. Tia was a thick chocolate chick! She had big breasts and ass for days. She had her thin hair cut into a bob. I'm just going to say this and leave it alone, thin hair does not belong in a bob. Megan was browned skinned, really small breasts and a big butt with her hair stopping right between her shoulder blades. The wheels in my head started turning immediately.

Candy dismissed the girls so they could take their showers and start getting ready. Candy explained the process to me. She had me crying laughing when she told me she makes them take showers before work every day to make sure they smell good and fresh. "Hey, I have to run to the mall. Do you need anything?" she asked me.

"Well, do you have all of your dancers' sizes?" I asked, making a list of things I wanted and for which dancer. She had already told me Raphael reimburses her for all out of pocket expenses pertaining to the club. After I gave her the list, she was out the door.

I ran out to my car because I needed to get the all black silk table cloths I bought earlier today. As I was bending over the trunk, I felt a strong pair of arms wrapping around me. Smiling and turning around because I already knowing who it was, I threw my arms around his neck. "What are you doing here babe? I told you I was fine," I said to him.

"You forgot I know you, huh?" he asked, standing there waiting on me to tell him. I gave him a brief run down on my conversation with Amere and how I felt about it. He kissed me and told me everything was cool.

"Babe!" I called out to him after a good idea hit me.

"Yea?" he asked while turning around.

"Can we get all of the girls sew ins? It will go with my classy theme. I also want to move them around out of their normal positions tonight. Do you think Raphael will mind?" I asked him.

"I'm sure he won't but I'll talk to him right now," he said.

"Okay, can you text me Candy's number? I need to text her my idea."

"Yea," he said before sending it to me.

Tamia: Hey Candy this is Tamia. I need scissors to cut hair. All the girls are going to get sew ins done for the party tonight. I have a lot of bundles in my car because I do hair on the side but I need to be able to cut their hair into the styles that fit their outfits.

Candy: Look at you! You sure you never done this before? LOL I got you tho

I smiled at her text message before carrying the bags of table cloths inside with me. I walked around cleaning each table before placing a silk black cloth on top of them. It took me several trips to the car for my glass centerpieces but with the help of Tony and even Roy, we got it covered within the hour. The centerpieces were shaped in the form of different animals of the jungle giving the place an animalistic feeling to it, while the tablecloth made it all presentable.

I walked back out to my car so I can get more cleaning supplies. It was time for me to sweep and mop then sanitize the bar area. On my way to the car, I couldn't help but feel like someone was watching me. I stopped and began looking around the parking lot but I didn't see anyone. This isn't the first time I've felt this way either. For the last four days, I've been feeling like someone is sitting back watching me but every time I look around, I never see anyone. Instead of brushing it off, I get my brass knuckles out of my purse and slide it in my pocket. After grabbing everything I needed, I headed back into the club to get started.

It took me two hours to get everything the way I wanted it and when I say this placed looked different and in an awesome way, there was no doubt about it! I sat down to rest my feet a bit.

I looked up just as Raphael and Rashard approached me. "Girl, you got this place looking like I need to charge more!" Raphael started laughing and looking around. "Are you employed?" he continued causing me to laugh.

"As much as I am enjoying this, it ain't something I want to do on the regular. The only bright side is I know I'm going to sleep good tonight. But you think you're impressed now? Wait til I finish with these ladies!" I said standing up.

"Where are you going babe?" Rashard asked.

"I have to go start on these sew ins before the doors open," I answered.

"Girl, Candy is on the last one and Michelle came in with her sew in done," he said. I was so confused because I didn't even see Candy come in at all! When I checked my watch, it was 6:30! "You fell asleep right here babe, so Candy started on the heads for you," he said after noticing how confused I was.

"Well, I have to go get dressed and link up with Deuce. I'll catch you when the party starts," he said before kissing my forehead and walking towards the side door. I promise I've never seen him coming or going until now.

I walked up to the DJ Booth doing one last check before I went to help the girls get dressed and cut their hair. While I was talking with the DJ, Michelle walked up to me. I didn't put two and two together when Rashard was saying her name a few minutes ago and I think we were both a little thrown off. She walked up while I was rearranging some things on the stage area and tried to tell me the stage doesn't go over here. I swear, this place has too many chiefs and not enough Indians. I was real polite about it though.

Anyway, my photographer arrived right on time. I had already explained to him over the phone where I wanted him to set up, so he went right to work. I went over to speak and then headed into the dressing room. "Candy, don't get offended but I'm going to go around and make sure everything is tight with their hair before I start cutting. Thanks for helping me and letting me get that sleep though," I said to her.

"No problem and I won't but don't you get offended either," she said, handing me a stick of gum. I started laughing so hard while popping it in my mouth. I didn't even think about brushing my teeth because I didn't realize I had fallen asleep.

After I styled everyone's hair, it was time to get them dressed and let them know their temporary job titles. I called Tammy up and helped her slide into her all white bustier crop top shirt. It had lace straps that crisscrossed down her stomach. Afterwards, I gave her a black tennis style mini skirt that flared out over her ass. It covered her booty completely but her thighs were exposed. Once she stepped into her stilettos, you couldn't tell her shit! She was so happy with her new look after she looked in the mirror, she gave me a hug. "You're going to be waitressing tonight, Tammy. The cages will be closed," I said to her. She just nodded her head and walked away still smiling.

Ashley walked up next to get dressed. She had a white T-shirt styled top but it was cut low, showing lots of cleavage. Her big titties didn't sag so I told her to take her bra off. She had no stomach so the shirt looked really good on her. It hugged her breast and showed her stomach. I finished her look off with short black shorts and really high heels. I wanted to draw attention to her breast and legs and it worked. "You will be bartending tonight," I said as she nodded her head before prancing off.

Both Tia and Megan had really bad shapes so it didn't matter what they had on. I wanted all of the girls in black and white but I wanted their outfits to be different. Tia wore a black tennis style dress that was tight at the top and flared out over her big butt. It was long enough so you couldn't see her ass but it was short enough to get your imagination running! She wore black stilettos as well. Now, Megan also wore a black dress! It fit her frame perfectly. The front of it was cut really low in the form of a V exposing the place between her breast and stopping at her navel. The back was made the same way, stopping in the middle of her back. I had no idea she had a tattoo in the center of her back of a lion! The tattoo alone made her dress the shit! The dress stopped about mid-thigh and had deep splits on both sides. Once she put on her heels, her and Tia thanked me before exiting the dressing room.

When I saw Michelle with her long weave and work attire, I had nothing to change about her. We had many conversations while she was my patient, so I knew she was extremely insecure. I didn't want to send her over the edge by changing anything.

I had completely forgotten about Tia when she walked up to me. Like I said before, she had no shape at all, so it was pretty hard thinking of something she could wear to make her look fuckable. She wore a white bra style bustier with black trimming and black shorts with white and black heels that crawled all the way up to her knees. I had cut her sew in into a bob and she looked amazing. I had already told Candy where I wanted the girls so once they were finished getting dressed, they all went to their posts.

Now it was time to work on me. I took a shower before lotioning my body. I threw on a simple two pieced red Vera Wang dress set that stopped at my knees. It was tight on my small breasts and left my stomach and back exposed by only connecting to the bottom half of the dress on the sides. The bottom of the dress flared out over my ass. I finished my look off with black fuck me pumps that were comfortable. After I finished getting dressed, I slid my brass knuckle on as an accessory. The club is dimly lit so no one will know right off what they are. I just can't shake the feeling that I'm being watched.

The crowd is finally coming in, and I notice Michelle and the chick from the hospital weren't together. The chick was sitting off in the cut watching. I'm not sure if she was watching me or just people watching, but I decided to keep a close eye on her.

I was having so much fun mixing and mingling with the crowd that I lost track of time. I have no idea why I was introducing myself like I would see these people again. A lot of them was asking if I could host a party for them the way I did for Deuce, but I politely told everyone this was a special favor. Nobody believed this was my first time. Raphael was so pleased with the club, dancers, and their positions for tonight that they may become permanent.

The commotion at the door caught my attention causing me to look towards the door. "Everybody get up and put ya hands together for da birthday boy, DEUCE!" I yelled over the microphone. Rashard's eyes and mine connected, making me melt. He winked at me and continued to walk in with Deuce. It was kind of hard for him to get all the way in because everybody was stopping him to tell him happy birthday and hugging him.

I was smiling until I saw Michelle approaching the wrong nigga with her arms open trying to get a hug. It was the wrong nigga because it ain't Rashard's birthday, but I'm the right bitch to take her outside and beat that ass for being disrespectful. I watched closely as he stepped out the way of her hug before whispering something in her ear. My blood started to boil until they both turned around and he pointed at me. When she turned and looked at me, she took off running. I have no idea what the two of them have going on but I'm for damn sure am going to find out.

Rashard walked up to me kissing me so passionately, everybody else disappeared. When he pulled away, I didn't even care about Michelle's ass no more. I was addicted to this man and we hadn't even had sex yet. "Get to work Miss Lady," he said to me before kissing me on my forehead.

I walked back up to the stage because I had a special surprise for the birthday boy. "Can I get the birthday boy to come up to the stage?" I asked over the microphone. He had so many hoes in his ear it was unbelievable and they all gave me an evil glare. I flashed a smile in their direction and turned to set the stage up for my surprise. I sat the microphone down and got Tony to hand me a chair. Of course, the birthday boy had to get a lap dance!

"Can I blindfold you?" I asked in his ear. He nodded his head grinning from ear to ear. Once he was blindfolded, I walked to the DJ Booth so I could tell him what to play. I looked out in the crowd and Rashard was looking at me quizzically, so I gave him a reassuring smile.

I turned around giving the DJ a head nod and the beat dropped. Ludacris started rapping as my girl made her way seductively to the stage.

"Catch me in the mall, you know I buy it out
G5 plane, yeah I fly it out
Ass on the back look like Lac sitting on28s
No you can't get her if you ain't got plenty cake
ATL, Georgia, booties look like this size
23 waist, pretty face, thick thighs"

The crowd went wild as she danced her way to the stage. I noticed Deuce's leg was shaking but I had to wait for the head nod. When she gave it to me, I removed the blindfold and Candy was on the stage dancing in front of him. She was wearing one of those all black masquerade masks with gold specks on it. She wore a black and gold panty and bra set from Victoria's Secret with the matching garter belt. Her all black stiletto heels had straps that crisscrossed all the way to her inner thigh, meeting the garter belt! She looked amazing and niggas were throwing money her whole way up to the stage.

"I can do it big, I can do it long
I can do it whenever or however you want
I can do it up and down, I can do circles
To him I'm a gymnast, this room is my circus
I market it so good, they can't wait to try-uh-uh-uh-uh me
I work is so good, man these niggas try to buy-uh-uh-uh-uh me
They love the way I ride it; they love the way I ride it
They love the way I ride it; they love the way I ride the beat

How I ride the beat
I ride it, they love the way I ride it
They love the way I ride it; they love the way I
ride the beat
Like a freak freak freak, uh"

Everybody was so focused on Candy and what she was doing that all we could hear was Ciara singing how these niggas love the way she rides it. Candy was most definitely doing the damn thing and when I looked at Deuce, he was mesmerized. She did a split and flipped backwards onto his lap while twerking. When she sat upright grinding to the beat, Deuce grabbed her hair pulling her head close to his face and licking her neck. By the time the song went off, I thought he was going to bend her over and fuck her right on the stage in front of everybody.

I grabbed her robe from the DJ and handed it to her, so she could go shower and get dressed to finish enjoying the party. Deuce's ass thanked me over and over. I continued to mingle with the guests but I didn't miss the daggers Michelle kept throwing at me with her eyes. I didn't care though, as long as she stayed over there, I wouldn't have to fuck her up.

After the party was over and everyone was leaving, I decided to go around collecting my table centerpieces. Raphael gave me a cart and a few boxes so I could make one trip. Rashard pushed the cart since he was walking with me. I opened my car door and couldn't believe my eyes! On my passenger seat there was a cup with 10 fingernails in it and a note attached to it. I grabbed the note so fast I almost knocked the cup over.

Dear bitch!

*you hoes thought you killed me huh? well bitch
you didn't!*
    see you soon

Check out these other great books from True Glory
Publications

Married To A Stranger

Daughter of Black Ice

Real Sisters

No Respect For A Weak Man 2

CPSIA information can be obtained
at www.ICGtesting.com
Printed in the USA
LVOW10s1854020317
525948LV00011B/767/P